I'D RATHER BE
A WITCH

ALSO BY ERIN HAYES

How to be a Mermaid
I'd Rather be a Witch
I Do Believe in Faeries (Coming March 2016)

The Harker Trilogy
Damned if I Do
Damned if I Don't (Coming January 2016)
Damned Either Way (Coming June 2016)

Death is but a Dream
Fractured
Jacob Smith is Incredibly Average

A Change of Heart (Coming February 2016)

Cover art by Lori Parker at Contagious Covers
Edited by Felicia A. Sullivan

AUTHOR'S NOTE

I'd Rather be a Witch is a spin-off standalone sequel to *How to be a Mermaid*. While you don't need to read *How to be a Mermaid* to enjoy this novella, there may be some terms at the beginning that may be unfamiliar, especially if you haven't seen the Weeki Wachee mermaids, and I highly recommend that you do!

I'd Rather be a Witch starts off with Jordyn being a part of a troupe of professional mermaids, humans who put on mermaid tails and perform water ballets in real life. Jordyn was a secondary character in *How to be a Mermaid*, and she was one of these professional mermaids.

This is Jordyn's story, which is completely different than Tara's from *How to be a Mermaid*. As you'll find out, there is a very real reason why Jordyn needed to be around water.

And you'll discover why, deep down, Jordyn would rather be a witch.

Enjoy!

For Chris, who put a spell on me ten years ago.

CHAPTER 1

TONIGHT, THERE WAS A BLOOD MOON IN LOS Angeles.

That was never a good thing. After all, I believe in bad omens.

You can't get me to cross the road when I see a black cat on the other side; I never open umbrellas inside; if I spill salt, I toss some over my shoulder; I always knock wood to counteract jinxes; and I have never liked Friday the thirteenth.

Those were only a few among many, many other bad omens that I was constantly aware of. When you're descended from a long line of witches, you don't mess with forces you don't fully understand. You have to respect them, because they certainly don't respect you. Even though I don't practice witchcraft anymore, I never ignore the signs.

When the clouds parted and I noticed the red moon for the first time, mocking me with its reminder of the last time I saw one, I wanted to scream.

I tried to mask my horror, but my friend and coworker, Alaina, still noticed. She was four months pregnant and had this supernatural ability to pick up on any change in emotions. Either that or I looked as horrified as I felt.

"Jordyn, what's wrong?" she asked.

The two of us were on West Washington Boulevard in Los Angeles, trying out some of the food trucks after a long day. Our professional mermaid troupe, Neptune's Mermaids, was in town for our exclusive water ballet performances at the L.A. Aquarium. We had sold out every show so far, and with another three performances in as many days, we were set to break our own records.

We were exhausted, and a kebab or some tacos sounded amazing.

At least they *did*. I had lost my appetite after seeing the moon.

"I—"

As soon as I started to speak, my phone rang. Even before I saw who was calling, I knew what it was going to be about: someone I loved had died or was dying. Because that's what blood moons meant in the past.

I answered the call, a sense of dread gripping me with icy tendrils.

"Hello?"

"Jordyn?" my little sister asked on the other end. When I heard the tears in her voice, I instantly felt them prick in the corners of my eyes. My heart pounded in answer, my mind screaming in time with it.

No, no, no, no.

"Yeah, Abby?"

"It's Mom. She's…" her voice trailed off before she spoke the words I didn't want to hear, because I already knew what they were going to be. "She got back from the doctor today. She…she has cancer."

I closed my eyes. "What kind?"

"Brain cancer." My sister's voice caught. "They say it's terminal. They've given her less than four weeks to live."

I covered my mouth with my hand, containing the cry that wanted to escape. Alaina saw my distress and frowned.

"Can you come home?" Abby asked. "I don't know what to do."

I nodded into the phone, not thinking about the other consequences of me returning home. Mom was all that mattered now. "I'll get there as soon as I can."

Abby only had one more word for me: "Hurry."

As I ended the call, I heard her gasping sob.

"I've got to talk to Neptune," I told Alaina, surprised at how strong my voice sounded. "I need to go home. My mother's sick."

Alaina's face crumpled into a sad frown. "Oh, Jordyn, I'm so sorry."

I may have messed up horribly in the past, but I certainly wasn't going to let my family down at a time like this.

After three years, it was finally time to go home.

***

"YES, OF COURSE YOU CAN TAKE SOME TIME off," my boss, Neptune, told me. We were sitting in the lobby of the hotel twenty minutes later, sipping on drinks from the café. My chamomile tea was doing nothing to calm my nerves. "Family is the most important thing."

Unfortunately, my absence meant that Neptune would have to cancel the remaining record-breaking shows in Lost Angeles. With only Alaina and Christine left, they couldn't do the full show.

Despite all my efforts to the contrary, I was bawling my eyes out, creating a scene in a public place.

I'd been numb after Abby called me, but once the tears started, I couldn't stop them. Somehow I managed to tell Neptune that my mother was dying, but beyond that, my words had quickly melted into blubbering.

"Buh—buh—but the shows... The muh—muh—money..."

"Aw, Jordyn, honey," Christine said, her voice cracking with sympathy. She wrapped me in a big hug. "It's going to be okay."

"Seriously," Alaina added. She hugged from my other side. "Your mom is way more important."

I gulped down some air, managing to get myself a little under control. "But you'd only have two mermaids for the show. How could—?"

Neptune shook his head. "Jordyn, we're in L.A., the city of actors, actresses, and everything in between. We'll find someone to replace you. You're not that special," he added playfully, which did the trick; I hiccupped a laugh. He didn't know my secret, that I actually *was* special. Or cursed, depending on your point of view. "Besides, since Tara left to go to college and Alaina is going to have her baby soon, we'll have to find more mermaids anyways. It's something we need to start doing. The troupe will be fine. Trust me."

I did trust him. I trusted Christine and Alaina, too, and even Tara, who had left the troupe a month ago to go to college full time. I didn't want to let them down, which was exactly what I was going to do. I'd been with them for two years and we'd gone through so much together. They were my family as much as my biological family.

"Jordyn," Christine said warmly, "don't worry about us. Just take care of your mother and your family, and everything will be fine."

Will it? Will a world without Mom still have bright and sunny days?

She brought all of that and more wherever she was. She took care of me, knew my failings and still loved me, even though one of my mistakes had splintered our family and destroyed another family. I was a bit of a freak by any standard, so losing one of the few people who understood me would leave me…

Lost.

"Thank you," I said, meaning it with every fiber of my being. "Thank you so much."

We hugged again, and Neptune joined in this time,

which was completely unlike him. I didn't care—I was so glad they were there for me. The kindness of my mermaid family made me cry harder, and that made Alaina cry harder.

I was going to miss them. Especially since I needed their strength more than anything. Now that I was going home, I'd have to face my past. Face *him*, Zachary Harington, the one person I never wanted to see again. The last time I saw him, he tried to kill me, and it was all my fault.

Because I was a witch who did one of the worst things imaginable in one moment of weakness.

I brought him back from the dead when we were seventeen.

CHAPTER 2

"FIRST TIME ON AN AIRPLANE?" THE MAN NEXT to me asked as the flight attendants went through their seat belt and floatation demonstrations. He smelled of bad B.O. and I breathed through my mouth.

Is the air conditioning broken? Could there be other mechanical failures in the plane?

I turned my face to him and shrugged weakly, trying not to let my imagination wander. "Something like that," I said noncommittally. Not quite a lie, but it was embarrassing to admit that I hated flying. I'd been traveling with Neptune's Mermaids for two years now, so I should be used to it by now. Right?

I wasn't. Not by a long shot.

"It's all right," the man said. "I still get nervous about and I've been doing it for decades now."

You're not helping. It also didn't help that I was in seat 13A. It was like the universe was trying to make me as uncomfortable as possible.

My hands made vice-like clamps on the ends of the armrests, as if I was trying to be one with the airplane seat.

My knees kept bobbing up and down, creating a chaotic drumbeat.

I was nervous as hell, like every time I flew. A witch who had an affinity for Earth-based magick has no business being in the air. Granted, an Earth-based witch has no business being a professional mermaid and spending most of her time around water, but that's exactly *why* I was a professional mermaid. It was to keep my elemental powers suppressed, and water was a far safer option. Fire was out of the question, obviously.

The man reached across me and closed the window shade, shielding me from a view of the outside and the ground. It was probably a good idea, considering that I probably would freak out once we were in the air.

"Just keep that closed," he said. "And think of something else."

"Thanks," I said through clenched teeth.

"Where are you headed?" he asked, trying to be conversational. "Or is DFW your final stop?"

"Jacksonville, Florida," I said, breathing heavily. "Centerburg, actually. About forty-five minutes outside of it."

The man leaned into me with a smile. "Business or pleasure?"

I felt the heat in my cheeks, mainly because I didn't want to focus on that either. "My mother's sick."

"Oh."

His face fell, catching most of my meaning in those

three words. But they didn't convey everything like how I didn't know what I was going to do if Mom was really dying. How would Abby take it? Who was going to help me in the future if I let my powers go wild again, other than my Great Aunt Margaret? I was sure she was still peeved at me for last time.

The truth was, I would be alone, and it was a reality that I didn't want to face.

"Sorry," my seat companion said.

"It's okay."

It's not okay.

I frowned and kept my eyes forward, trying to keep my mind off the sense of impending doom that flying gave me.

The flight attendants finished their demonstrations, and the plane lurched forward. Two trips in the air and I'd be at Mom's side and there for Abby.

Millions of people flew every day, and millions of those made it to their final destination, even if they did sit in row 13. Not too many died on the way. I had to keep telling myself that.

My stomach floundered as we turned. Were we about to take off?

Focus on something else.

Except, when I thought about anything else, my mind either jumped to my mother on her deathbed or to my ex-boyfriend Zach, who I knew was waiting for me.

Zachary Harington and I grew up as neighbors on

our quiet street in Centerburg, Florida. Other than his older brother and my younger sister, we were the only kids in the entire neighborhood with only creepy Old Mr. Samson's house between our two houses. As kids, we'd run as fast as we could to each other's homes, trying to avoid Mr. Samson's ever-watchful glaring eyes.

The old man's house looked like it had been built with craft sticks forty years ago and gave off a creepy haunted vibe. Not that our houses were all that much better. We lived in an older neighborhood that hadn't been kept up over the decades. My family had been there for a long time, and my Great Aunt Margaret even lived in a house five down from ours. "To make sure we don't get into trouble," was her reasoning for living so close.

It was home. And even what happened couldn't change how wonderful my childhood was.

Zach and I would play house, dragging poor Abby into it. Even then, at the age of three, before my parents divorced and shattered my idea of a perfect family, I knew which man I wanted for a husband.

It had always been Zach.

After playing house, he'd always insist we'd go to his house and play video games. It had to be boring for his older brother, Luke, but he always let us play two player games together. Granted, I wasn't any good at it, yet that was kind of the joke and what made it fun.

Then Zach and I hit elementary school and he got pulled aside to his group of friends. I was immediately labeled as a witch and subsequently barred from having any friends. No one wanted to be friends with the girl whose family was a bunch of witches. For generations, we were ostracized from society. The cops were constantly at our doorstep every time a neighborhood pet went missing. If summers ran too hot, people blamed us; if it was too wet and cold, they did the same. Like we didn't have better things to do than ruin the weather for our town.

You would have thought we were in Salem, Massachusetts in the 1600s. But no, we were in Northern Florida, present day. Like my superstitions, you can't get people to stop bad habits, especially when it came to pointing the finger at us.

Yet that was life as I knew it. Still, I was unprepared for being outcast by everyone in school. Kids and teachers alike snubbed me, called me names, and said too many bad things to count.

It was a very lonely time in my life, one that I spent with my nose in a book or trying to cast spells to give my tormentors a bad case of the chicken pox. Mom grounded me when she found out that I tried that, especially since it worked more than once.

Up until then, I'd always had my best friend with me. And then he wasn't. It wasn't that Zach took part in ridiculing me—in fact, I think he defended me most of the time. Still we did go our separate ways all through middle school. He played football and I was the girl who hid behind her curtain of brown hair, who worked on her

Book of Shadows and practiced her craft at home.

When we hit high school though, everything changed.

Zach asked me out. And I said yes.

I don't know if it was because he was the running back for the football team or what, but he was immune to the stigma that dating me held. In fact, it propelled me into the spotlight. Suddenly people who, before, wouldn't give me the time of day were talking to me, including me.

Zach and I were in love, together as soul mates. He was my first kiss. He was my only lover. We would probably still be together if the worst hadn't happened.

It was junior prom night. Sure, they always make a big deal out of senior prom, but junior prom was magickal for me.

Trust me, I know magick.

It was everything they said prom would be. We danced. We laughed. We hung onto each other like we were the only people in the universe. It was only him and me.

And that was perfect.

After the dance ended at midnight, Zach drove me out to Shady Point, a forested area on the outskirts of town.

"What are we doing, Zach?" I asked with a giggle. I had sneaked my first taste of champagne and I was feeling a bit bubbly.

"We're going for a walk," Zach said, linking his fingers through mine as he coaxed me out of the car. Those clear blue eyes of his were bright and full of hope that night.

He'd been entirely mindful to not take a sip of alcohol since he was driving.

Zach had always been considerate like that.

We wove through the trees, taking a less-travelled path through the woods. As soon as we reached our destination, I grinned at him. "You're taking me to the Peak?"

He laughed. "I guess it's cliché, right?"

"No, it's perfect." Cliché or not, this was exactly how I pictured my prom night.

The Peak, as it was locally known, was the highest point in Centerburg, an outcropping of rocks that overlooked the town. While he was still in his tux and I in my princess gown, we sat on the edge of the Peak, and watched the lights below.

"It's beautiful," I whispered.

"You're beautiful."

I was about to protest with some quip when he caught my lips with his, pulling me to him. I always got lost in his kisses. They cast a spell over me, binding my thoughts, making me bend to their power. I didn't mind.

He was all that I wanted.

"You were saying?" he rumbled as our lips parted.

"You're wonderful."

Hand in hand, we lay on the grass, looking up at the cloudy night sky, talking about everything and nothing. It was like that with him. We connected like two puzzle pieces, interlocked in our pasts and our futures.

As I watched the sky, I saw the clouds part, revealing

the full moon. It was red.

A blood moon.

I recoiled, rolling away from him, breaking the connection between our fingertips.

"What is it?" he asked.

"Let's head back," I told him uneasily. "It's getting late."

"Okay."

Zach never questioned me when I got a bad vibe. He was used to my little freakouts. After a lifetime of knowing me, he knew that I flipped out when I spilled the salt or a broom fell. It was all a part of my being a witch, and he respected that.

I tried not to hurry him too much to head back to the car, but it felt like we weren't moving fast enough. The blood moon haunted me like some sort of specter, laughing at me the entire way.

"Jordyn?" Zach asked me. "Are you all right?"

"Yes," I lied. "Hurry."

Maybe I should have told him more. Maybe warning him would have saved him. I could tell that I had worried him though, and I didn't want to make him worry.

Our car came into view, and I sobbed in relief. By then, I was hysterical for fear of what *could* happen.

"Almost there," I panted, practically dragging him along at that point.

"Jordyn?"

I turned to look at him and saw the concern etched

in his face as he looked down at me. I remembered the way he looked that night, so polished and handsome in his tux, his hair a bit messed up from laying on the ground. The light of the moon silhouetted his face and I could tell in that moment that he loved me.

What was more, I loved him back.

Then the light on his right side grew stronger with yellow beams of light. Another car. I turned my head to see the hulking piece of metal hurtling towards him. Too fast for the forested area. Too fast to stop.

The car's headlights blinded me, and I was unable to see anything else about it. I couldn't tell if it was a sedan, a truck, or some other sort of vehicle. In my dreams, it was a monster.

In reality, it was a murder weapon.

The driver of the car laid on its horn, filling the night with the awful noise. When it impacted with Zach's body, it sounded even worse. It hit him head on, missing me completely. It threw him up and over the hood, his body rolling like a broken ragdoll over the metal.

I screamed.

Zach landed on the ground in a heap while the vehicle peeled away. The headlights had blinded me so much I couldn't see a license plate, if there had even *been* a license plate. My only concerned in that moment was Zach.

"Zach!" I screamed, kneeling next to him. "Zach!"

Tears obscured my vision, which was probably for the best. There was too much blood and so many ways his limbs were twisted and banged up. His head was cracked open, and I could see into his skull.

Worst of all, he wasn't breathing and he wouldn't respond to anything I was shouting at him.

"Please wake up, Zach! *Please?*" I was desperate, shaking him, trying to get any sort of response.

My phone was in the car, left behind so that we could have our private moment on the Peak. I didn't want to leave him to get it, but if I didn't, I couldn't call the ambulance.

I knew it was too late to save him in any case.

Tears stained my face as I looked down at my first love, and I made a decision. One that used forbidden magick. My Great Aunt Margaret had always told me to be careful about the magick that I used. She said that I was a strong witch, one of the strongest that my family had seen in over two hundred years, and that I needed to only use white magick for good.

She made me promise, because bad things happened when we dabbled in dark magick.

I sat there with the knowledge that my white, Earth-based magick wouldn't bring back my Zach. White magick wouldn't undo this tangled mess of limbs and blood. If he didn't live, *I* couldn't live.

In that desperate moment, I made a decision to break my promise to Aunt Margaret.

My instincts took over, and my actions weren't my own.

Still, I have only myself to blame for what happened

next.

I drew a pentagram in the dirt next to Zach. Usually a spell like this required goat's blood, but I instinctively knew I'd be fine. I tried not to think too much about rolling his body over on the center of the pentagram. Tried not to hear his broken limbs creak or pay attention to the amount of blood that he spilled.

He was going to be fine after this. He had to be, or else I'd go crazy.

I frantically tore open the shirt of his tux, bit my palm until it bled, and then drew another pentagram on his chest, my blood mingling with his.

I muttered the incantation that came to my mind—I have no idea where it came from, only that it appeared in my mind. It would work. It had to.

I repeated the phrase over and over, summoning every ounce of energy and strength that I had. Desperation intertwined with my own Earth-based gifts, strengthening them, turning my power into something that I didn't recognize. The Earth called to me, beckoning my talents. I called upon an element that was older than time, and it *responded back*.

I felt the shock in the air before I saw the change. All at once, I heard rustling in the trees and the distinct sound of still little bodies hitting the dirt.

It took me a moment to figure out what they were: in order to bring him back to life, I had to take life, only I didn't realize that it would be every living thing in a twenty-foot radius around us. Dead birds, squirrels, and even bugs littered the ground around me, their life essence used up by the spell.

I looked around in horror, realizing what I'd done. This wasn't me. This wasn't the kind of witch I was.

My heart pounded in my ears and I covered my mouth in horror. What had I done?

Then, through all the numbness that threatened to consume me, I felt a caress on my cheek, bringing me back to stark reality.

I looked down at Zach, sobbing now that I saw his eyes open. His head was no longer a gaping mess, and his bones had knitted back together, giving him the semblance of being a complete person.

"Jordyn," he said, his voice sounding like dry, rustling leaves. "Why are you crying?"

I did it for him.

"Zach!"

I sobbed and hugged him close. I kissed his once-dead lips, still cold, still a bit stiff, but very much alive. He was going to be all right. He was alive, and this was going to be some sort of horrible memory that I would laugh about in a few years' time.

With him.

Because he was alive.

"Why are you crying?" he asked again.

"I thought I'd lost you."

I called an ambulance, because there was no other way

to explain the state of his clothes or what had happened that night. They took him to the hospital where I met my mom, Abby, and his family.

The doctors were shocked. Other than a few bumps and bruises, including one to his head that they were concerned about, he was relatively unharmed. They did want to keep him overnight for observation in case there was something wrong internally.

I made a statement to the police about the car that hit him, but I'd been so traumatized, I couldn't remember what it looked like, only that there had been *something* that hit him at a high speed. Nothing ever came out of it. I suspect that, despite Zach's family's protests, the police didn't look too hard for the mysterious car.

After all, Zach was unharmed and fine. Or so we thought.

I sat with Zach in the hospital the next morning, holding his hand while the doctor did one last once-over before releasing him. Zach looked back at me, our eyes connecting. And he smiled.

I froze.

Those aren't his eyes.

Before, Zach had clear blue eyes, like a cloudless day in the summertime. Now they were a dull blue, almost gray. Not only that, his pupils were depthless, like a shark's eyes. They seemed to suck the light from around us into those twin black holes. Something slithered behind them, something unnatural. I didn't know what it was, but I knew that it wasn't Zach.

"What's wrong?" he asked in a light tone.

"Nuh—nothing," I answered.

Everything felt wrong.

It started with little pebbles hitting my window at 3am about a week later. I lived on the second floor of my house, so when I went to the window, it was about a twenty-foot drop to see who was below me.

"Zach?" I asked dumbly, recognizing his shape below me.

He was fully dressed, like he hadn't been to bed at all. He turned his face up towards me, his black hole eyes glittering like coins in the moonlight. They had gotten worse in the time since he died.

"Hey," he said. "What are you doing?"

I crossed my arms across my breasts, not realizing even then that I was putting myself in a defensive posture. Subconsciously, I knew he was dangerous. Consciously, I was denying that he wasn't my Zach. "Trying to sleep, Zach. You should be doing the same."

"Couldn't sleep," he said, although I got the impression that he hadn't even tried. "Can't stop thinking about you."

Despite everything, that statement made my heart break. "Why, Zach?"

"Because I love you."

He'd never said it so freely before, but when he did, I could feel all of the power of his emotions behind it. Now, when he said those three words to me, it felt hollow and empty. Like someone else was saying them.

I shivered. "I love you, too," I said, meaning it, but for the Zach I knew before. "But you need to go back to bed. You're still healing up from the accident."

"I'm fine, Jordyn. Can I come up?" He rubbed at his head. "It's just…you're up *here*. In my head. And I can't get you out of it. The only way is to be around you. I need help. I want you to help me."

I paused, my heart breaking for him, and then I shook my head. "You really should get back to bed. We'll talk in the morning."

I turned away from his protests. It broke my heart to do so, but something told me not to go down and see him.

That wasn't Zach.

He wouldn't give up though. He threw more pebbles at my window, his shouting getting more and more violent until one sizable rock crashed through the glass. That finally alerted my mom who, at my terrified appearance, told Zach that she'd call the police if he didn't leave. I lied, telling her that I had no idea why Zach was acting strangely. She bought my excuses. I think.

It didn't stop there.

With only three weeks left before summer break, Zach skipped his classes to follow me around everywhere, including sitting in on my classes. He followed me home from school, he waited in his car out in front of the house, keeping his ever-watchful eyes trained on it, waiting for any sign that I'd be coming out. He quit going to football practice, he stopped going to his after school job at the Piggly Wiggly.

His only purpose in life became me. It terrified me, because I didn't recognize this new Zach.

I wasn't the only one who noticed that Zach was acting strange. His mother asked me what had happened to make him act so out of character, and all I could say was that he was traumatized from the ordeal.

Even Zach's older brother was concerned.

"What happened that night, Jordyn?" Luke asked me in despair. Luke looked so much like the way Zach *used* to and it hurt my heart. "He's not acting like the brother I know at all."

No he wasn't. Unfortunately, I couldn't tell him the truth, that I had brought Zachary Harington back from the dead and he was obsessed with me.

To make it even worse, nothing came out of the investigation about who attacked us that night, or even if it *was* an attack. That particular moment in time didn't exist outside of what it had done to Zach. I had nightmares about it and tried spells to help me recall what happened. The cops dismissed it as an accidental hit and run.

I knew better.

Still, life has a way of marching on.

I started having nightmares about Zach's obsession of me. I'd wake up in a sweat and go to the window, only to find that he was actually outside, staring up at me.

Then dead, mutilated squirrels started appearing on the front porch of my house, like Sadie, our white cat, was leaving us presents. It was something we had seen before, only these appeared more frequently, and when we didn't acknowledge it, the dead animals started getting larger and larger. When one of our neighbors' Labradors showed up dead on our doorstep, I got desperate for it to stop.

That night, when I saw him take his watch below my window, I grabbed a protection charm and ran downstairs, determined to end this once and for all. For his stoic demeanor, Zach immediately brightened up when I opened the door.

He beamed at me with a smile that didn't quite reach his eyes. "Jordyn. You came."

"You have to stop. You have to go back home, go to sleep, and *be normal*. Please."

He shook his head. "I can't, Jordyn. Not with you in here." He tapped his temple. "And in here." He tapped his heart.

That broke mine even more. "You don't want that. You need to go be yourself. Live your life." I swallowed thickly. "I'll still be here for you."

I wasn't sure if that was true or not. I was completely terrified by the entire experience, and I didn't know if my being around was healthy or not. I still loved him—but I loved the old Zach, not this shell that looked and sounded like him. If anything, I loathed this version of him. I didn't want to be scared anymore. I wanted my life back. I wanted *his* life back.

Somehow he picked up on it.

He moved towards me threateningly. "You don't love me, do you?" he raged.

"Zach, I—"

"You don't love me anymore!"

His hands flew to my neck and squeezed, choking me, crimping my air passages until there was no more airflow. My eyes bulged and my vision darkened. I beat at his arms, trying to get him to let go of me, but they were iron clamps.

"Now, when I need you, you want to abandon me!"

He was going to kill me. The protection charm was the only thing that kept him from crushing my larynx like a walnut in an instant.

"What the—?"

Over the thundering of my blood pumping through my ears, I heard my mother yell my name. Then another voice yelled an incantation. A blast of energy hit Zach full in the chest, pushing him away from me. I sobbed a breath, sweet air filling my lungs.

Abby's fingers touched my shoulder, giving me strength.

"Jordyn!" Mom asked. "Are you okay, honey?"

My Great Aunt Margaret stood in front of me, forcing herself between Zach and me. I have no idea why she was over at my house that night, but she saved my life.

I really thought I was going to die. I may have if

Aunt Margaret hadn't stopped him.

"Go, Zachary," she urged. "Go, before I call the cops."

Zach's eyes met mine one last time, a menacing power in them that promised so many terrible things. I knew that the next time we saw each other, he wouldn't let me go.

He ran into the night.

Aunt Margaret whirled on me, angry and frightened at the same time. "What did you do to him?" she demanded.

"What?"

"There's a curse on him," Aunt Margaret told my mother, her voice angry. "I can smell it."

Mom stepped away from me, a look of horror on her face. "What happened, Jordyn?"

Between my tears and my terror at seeing Zach like this, I told them. I didn't hold anything back.

Mom listened intently, her mood changing to horror when I went into the details of what I had done that terrible night. At some point, Abby joined us. I couldn't help but think how lucky she was not to be gifted with magick; she'd never be tempted to do something like this.

When I finished, the four of us sat in silence, mourning the passing of the Zach that once was and wondering what we could do with the Zach that remained.

"What do I do?" I asked. "I love him so much, but this…this isn't him. This isn't right."

"Margaret?" Mom asked, turning to our aunt for answers. "What should we do?"

Aunt Margaret gave me a hard look, weighing our options. "We can't do away with him," she said at length. "That's another wrong that won't right this problem." She combed her fingers through her gray hair. "I always told you that you were a powerful witch, Jordyn. I just didn't know you'd stoop to something like this."

Her words shattered what remained of my heart. "He was dead. I couldn't let him die like that."

Mom caressed my shoulders, giving me strength in that simple movement.

"I understand why you did it," Aunt Margaret continued. "But it still wasn't right."

"Can't we undo it?" I asked, despite the fact that the thought was terrible. At that point, I just wanted him to be at peace. "Or, maybe, we can exorcise him of whatever's causing him to do this?"

"I don't think there's a way we can undo it," Mom said sadly, looking to Aunt Margaret for advice. "That means that we have to deal with the aftermath now."

"Which is?" Abby asked.

Aunt Margaret sat back, wheels turning in her head as she weighed all of the options. "I'll look into it," she said cryptically. "A banishing spell to send him away. Or a binding spell."

"We'll both look into it," Mom added fiercely.

Mom was always protective like that. It helped me through the worst times in my life, and this was certainly one of the worst.

My mother and aunt locked themselves up in our family's library, poring over spell books and my ancestors' *Books of Shadows*. As far as I knew, they were trying spells, tweaking them, and trying desperately to find a solution. If anyone could figure it out, they could.

Meanwhile, I confined myself to the house and didn't go to school, too afraid to leave in case Zach was somewhere around, waiting for me. It was like I was in prison to keep myself safe.

Abby stayed with me, which helped ground me and keep me sane. In those dark days, my little sister was my only friend.

After three days, Mom and Aunt Margaret emerged from the library, looking exhausted. Mom had a sickly pallor to her skin that spoke of the toll it had taken on her. Her eyes were sad and hollow as she looked at me.

"What happened?" I asked.

"We tried," Aunt Margaret replied tersely. "We failed."

Fingers of dread clenched my stomach. "So what do we do?"

My great aunt sighed and leveled her gaze at me. "We can't take care of him directly, but if you were far away, he may be able to recover. He may be more himself. Right now, you dominate his thoughts whenever you're near. You're the one who brought him back. You're the one he wants to be around. So we need to separate you two."

Next to me, Abby's entire body went rigid. "But that

means…" Tears filled her eyes.

Mom looked at me sadly and she started crying as well.

Horror joined dread and tumbled about in my stomach. Bile lurched in my throat. "There's got to be something else," I whispered.

"Jordyn," Mom said. She wouldn't meet my eyes, but I'll never forget how desolate she looked in that one moment. "You're going to have to leave us."

"And what?" I asked. "I'm …exiled? What about you? Can't you come with me?"

Mom looked like she was ready to jump with me and leave Centerburg and all of this behind, then Aunt Margaret stepped between us.

"We'll have to stay here," she said gravely. She gestured between herself, Mom and Abby. "To keep an eye on him and see if there's any other way to bind him. If you're gone, he may be able to move on. But we need to make it as easy as possible on him. He's in a fragile state at the moment."

My own tears started then.

"I promise," Aunt Margaret swore. "I promise we'll find something to bring you back to us, Jordyn."

There was no way of making it easy on anyone. I'd have to leave my world behind, they'd be losing me, and Zach would be losing his obsession.

I tried reasoning with them, begged them to come along with me. We could start a new life together somewhere else. But Aunt Margaret insisted that *ceteris paribus*, everything had to remain the same for Zach to reacclimatize to his new existence. They had to remain where they were. They'd still look for a cure or a binding spell, something to keep him from turning more into this psychotic being I barely recognized.

I'd lose everything. In a sick, twisted way, it was worse than losing Zach that one night, all because of the decision I made in a fit of a sorrow.

I vowed then to never use my magick ever again, because it ruined lives. It hurt the ones I loved, and I would never do anything like that to them ever again.

Deep in the depths of my sorrow, I decided to burn my *Book of Shadows* in a gesture of completely letting go of who I was. I threw it in the fireplace and watched the flames eat the crumbling pages through my tears. I didn't lose just any book that night—I lost a piece of my soul. My identity.

It was a sacrifice I was willing to make in order to keep this from happening again. Now I wasn't a witch. I was Jordyn Murphy, who had no idea who she was any more.

Except for being a screw up.

I broke up with Zach through a letter that I left in his mailbox. I agonized over the words for the longest time, finally deciding that something short was all that I could say because there weren't enough words in the world to tell him how sorry I was and how much I wish I could fix him.

I'm leaving to find life elsewhere. I hope you do too, Zach. I loved you and I always will. But we need to go our separate ways. It's for the best.

It's for the best. That became my mantra, four words that I've lived by for the last three years. It certainly didn't feel like "the best" for the longest time.

I dropped out of high school and completed my GED online. I moved to Jacksonville, still within reach of Centerburg, but far enough way that I didn't impact Zach's life. I joined the mermaids at Neptune's World. Being around another element like water caused my connection with Earth to fade and get fuzzy in my mind, making me unable to draw on it as much. It was exactly what I needed. As a bonus, it enabled me to move around the country whenever we toured, making me a moving target. I couldn't have asked for a better opportunity.

I made good money as a mermaid and I took online courses to be a nurse, since I naturally leaned toward healing.

Mom and Aunt Margaret kept searching for a spell, any sort of reprieve, and I did my own searching online, although I wouldn't experiment. I wasn't a witch. Not anymore.

Nothing ever came out of it though, and there was no hope for curing Zach, so I never went back to Centerburg.

Until now.

Because Mom's dying.

I was jolted awake as the wheels of the plane struck the ground, shaking me like a maraca. I took in a shuddering breath, and my companion next to me grinned.

"We made it to DFW," he said. "Good luck on your journey."

Yeah. Of course. One more flight and I'd be in Jacksonville.

I wondered if Zach would sense that I'd be near him. After all, it had been three years since I left, so maybe the side-effects of my ill-considered spell had worn off a bit.

Who was I kidding? I dreaded what lay ahead.

CHAPTER 3

TO MY RELIEF, I WAS SEATED IN 27C ON MY second flight and the plane landed in Jacksonville on time and in one piece. You would have thought that after my first flight I'd have more of a handle on my paranoia, but I didn't. It wasn't until we pulled up to the gate that I felt like I wasn't going to die.

I texted Christine that I had landed safely in Jacksonville. She'd always been the one to hold my hand when we took off and landed, something I sorely missed on this trip.

The woman sitting next to me on this flight hadn't been anywhere near as chatty as the guy from LAX to DFW, and it allowed me to keep to myself and plan out different scenarios for when and if I did see Zach again. Basically, my plan was to go home and hide as much as possible.

Pathetic, I know.

I only had my carry-on, so I was able to walk right out to the ground transportation area. I dialed Abby as I put my jacket on. Jacksonville felt a bit colder than Los Angeles.

"Hey, I'm here," I told her when she answered, trying to sound as cheery as possible.

"Hey," Abby replied, her voice exhausted. She sounded preoccupied. "Listen, Mom had a bad morning and was sick, so I asked a friend to pick you up at the airport."

I blinked. "A friend? Who did you—?"

"Hey, stranger," a familiar-yet-unfamiliar voice said. I turned at the sound of the voice and froze when I saw who it was. "I think your 'friend' just found me," I told Abby in the phone. "I'll see you in an hour."

I hung up and stared dumbfounded at the person who spoke.

"Luke?" I asked, shocked.

It was Luke, Zachary's older brother. The other boy I'd spent most of my early life with.

He grinned at me, his hands stuffed into his jean pockets. "Long time, no see, Jordyn."

"It's been a long time."

I almost didn't recognize him. This wasn't the Luke that I remembered from three years ago. That Luke had an extra bit of weight on him from having his nose buried in books instead of running around outside. Not that he'd been fat, he just didn't have the physique of an athlete. Not like he did now.

Luke had been bespectacled and riddled with acne. While Zach had been on track to be a pro athlete, Luke was the smart one, the one who would go to college and find the cure for cancer.

This version of Luke was someone entirely different.

This one was some sort of heartthrob, with his tanned skin, blue eyes, and short brown hair. I gawked at him, unable to reconcile this new version of Luke Harington with the one I grew up with. Zach wasn't the only one who'd had a big change in his family; Luke had become a different person in that time.

He chuckled, clearly pleased at my reaction.

"Surprised?" He gave me a mischievous, lopsided grin, one that I'm sure was illegal in a few counties.

"Yeah. You look…" I struggled for the appropriate word. "You look *good.*"

"So do you," he said with that smile. "Your hair's pink now."

"It was actually red, then it faded. I wanted to look like Ariel from *The Little Mermaid.* All the kids wonder why we don't look like Ariel."

He smirked. "Abby told me about the mermaid thing. It's certainly interesting."

"I enjoy it a lot."

Sensing my somber mood, Luke gestured towards the parking lot. He took my backpack from my hands and shouldered it. "Let's get going," he said. "I'll take you home, then I have to report to work at two o'clock."

Does Zach know that I'm here?

Luke led me to his car, a Toyota Prius, in one-hour parking. Nothing too flashy, but that's how Luke had always been. He'd always been content to be his own person.

Except now he was an entirely different person. This was so confusing.

He put my bag in the trunk while I settled into the passenger's side. I was tired, yet oddly wired. Apparently, this trip was going to be filled with unexpected surprises.

"Thanks for picking me up," I said as he slid into the driver side. I took my jacket off and stuffed it in the back. "I'm sorry if it's been a pain in the ass."

Centerburg was nearly an hour away. I hadn't considered who would have had to pick me up if Abby couldn't.

Luke buckled his seatbelt. "It's no problem. After all, it gave me the chance to say hi to you after so long."

"You used to pick me up in middle school when it rained, remember that?" I added with a grin. Back then, Luke had just gotten his driver's license, so it was especially nice of him to pick up the weird girl when no one else would give me rides.

Luke's cheeks flushed. "Yeah."

"I'm sorry I haven't been back in—"

"Three years," he finished for me. He turned on the car. "It's been three years since you left."

"How have you been?"

He let out a breath before he reversed out of the spot. "Tired," he admitted.

Mom and Abby had told me that Zach had quieted down after I left, that the killing spree of the animals on our doorstep had lessened and then stopped altogether. They didn't see much of Zach, but he wasn't as violent as he once was, and supposedly he still lived at home.

However, that wasn't an indication of what had happened behind closed doors at the Harington household.

"How has…" I struggled for a moment, unsure if I really wanted to ask this question or not. To Luke, I was the girl who broke his kid brother's heart. "How has Zach been?"

"He's been…*better*," Luke said in a tone that didn't make me think he was *really* better. "He's trying to go to college again."

"Trying?"

"Yeah."

Maybe I shouldn't have asked about Zach. This was too painful.

"I'm glad he's better," I offered.

"So'm I." Luke kept his eyes trained on the road. "He's living with Mom and Dad at home. Going to therapy, trying to work out some issues. So yeah. He's better."

I clenched my fists in my lap and blinked back tears. I had ruined his family's lives. Why Luke would ever want to have anything to do with me or even exchange two words with me ever again, I had no idea.

"What about you?" I asked finally, changing the subject. My voice sounded a bit strangled, but Luke didn't appear to notice.

"Well," he said at length. "I became a cop."

It took a moment for that to sink in.

"Wait, what?" I exclaimed. "You became a cop? As in a policeman?"

"Yep."

"When did *that* happen?"

He let out a breath, frowning slightly. "Shortly after you left, I guess."

"I never knew you wanted to be a cop," I said. "I always thought you wanted to be a doctor. Or something."

"Well," he said, flicking his eyes over me. "I wanted to do something immediate for the community, because there's still some bad people out there, and some questions left unanswered."

The muscles in his jaw clenched and unclenched, the only sign of the conflicting feelings for his younger brother.

He's doing this for Zach. He wants to find out who ran him down.

I don't know what came over me then, but I put my hand over his on the armrest and gave it a quick squeeze. "I'll bet crime has gone down since you started."

Centerburg was never really a dangerous place, but it did have its armed robberies and violent crimes. It was a great place for us to grow up as kids. Childhood was one of those things you always remembered through rose-colored glasses. We'd had a good childhood together, even with everyone calling me a witch.

"Well, you know, we try our best."

"I'm sure you kick ass."

He chuckled mirthlessly at that. "Possibly. I don't know." He shrugged and I laughed in response. "So how is being Ariel going?"

"Being a professional mermaid, you mean?" I teased. He nodded. "Well, it's been a lot of fun."

I told him about my time as a professional mermaid, especially since it lightened the mood in the car. I told him about visiting all the different cities during the tour. I told him about the one Beluga whale at Neptune's World that always tried to flirt with me whenever we did a performance at our home aquarium.

To Luke's credit, he did appear genuinely interested in my story, asking questions about certain things, wondering what we did at each aquarium. Admittedly, I liked to go into great detail about my job, and he didn't appear to mind.

I missed this—being able to really talk with someone who knew me from before.

I noticed at one point when we went to extremely familiar territory. After three years, Centerburg had evolved. There were more strip malls, more construction on the roads to allow for the increase in traffic. And it looked like there were a lot more cars on the roads. When we passed by certain housing developments, I saw that residential areas had started to sprout up like daisies.

They say you can never go home again, and it's true. I was in some sort of pseudo-rendition of the town that I had grown up in.

"It's changed so much," I remarked as the scenery passed.

Luke followed my gaze and nodded. "A lot has happened in three years."

"Yes," I agreed. "A lot."

I wondered what I'd find when I got home.

CHAPTER 4

WE PULLED UP TO THE FRONT OF MY HOUSE. It looked smaller and older than I remembered, but three years could do that to a place, I guess. Mr. Samson's house sat beside mine on the right and beyond that was the Harington house, where Zach inevitably was watching. Five houses down was Aunt Margaret's house, although I wasn't sure if I was looking forward to seeing her. The disappointment in her voice the last time I saw her was enough to make me squirm.

I gulped down some air. I imagined Zach's eyes boring through the car to watch me. No, that was all in my head. I couldn't think that way, not while I was here, otherwise I was going to drive myself crazy. My life was crazy enough.

The thought occurred to me that I should have told Luke to pull around the back, so there would be less of a chance for Zach to spot me. I'd been so transfixed by the change in Centerburg that it had completely escaped my mind until it was too late.

By then, I saw that someone else had been waiting for me.

"Jordyn!" Abby cried. She bounded down the steps and jogged the rest of the way to the car.

I got out just in time for her to throw her arms around me and wrap me up in a bear hug, her body shaking with sobs. The last time I saw her was last Christmas in Jacksonville, and in that time, she'd grown up into a beautiful seventeen-year-old, the same age I was when I brought Zach back from the dead. Hopefully, she doesn't share my disposition for breaking the rules, although she was blessed without the gift for magick, so she wouldn't get into as much trouble as I did.

"I'm so glad you're here," she sobbed into my shoulder. "Mom is…"

"Shh," I crooned, holding her close. I smoothed her hair down and squeezed her tightly, never wanting to let her go. "I'm here now."

Luke came around, carrying my bag from the trunk. I gave him a nervous glance, unsure of what to do with him idly standing there with my luggage. *Should I invite him in?* I wasn't sure about the state of the house, or if we had anything to offer him.

Abby composed herself, taking in a deep breath. She turned her watery eyes on Luke. "Thanks for picking her up, Luke," she said, her voice catching. "Mom's…"

"I completely understand," Luke said gently, giving her one of those swoon-inducing, lopsided smiles. He glanced at me. "Besides, I enjoyed the opportunity to catch up with Jordyn."

"Jordyn? Is that you?"

At the sound of the man's voice behind me, I froze, thinking that it was Zach. It was ridiculous, because the voice sounded far too old to be him. Still, my instincts took over and my entire body seized up in fear.

"Yes it is, Mr. Samson," Abby called out wearily. "She's only visiting."

If I could have melted into a puddle on the ground with relief, I would have. I turned around and gave a weak wave to the man watching us from the porch of the house next door. It was Mr. Samson, our next-door neighbor. Even though he was probably in his only in his late sixties, I always thought of him as a really old man that didn't appear to have any hobbies other than watering his lawn.

"Hi, Mr. Samson," I said. "Hope you're well."

"Been a while," the old man snapped. "And your hair is an unnatural color. Unnatural like your whole family."

Did I mention that I didn't like my neighbor? He was one of those old men that yelled at kids to stay off his lawn. A real charmer.

"Thanks, Mr. Samson," I said. I put my arm around Abby's shoulders and started ushering everyone inside. I didn't want to be out here longer than I had to be. Mr. Samson had already spotted me; I'd be surprised if Zach wasn't far behind.

Once inside, my white cat came running into the foyer, her legs moving with the speed of Scooby Doo. She never used to show affection like this. I guess she missed me.

"Sadie!" I cried, kneeling down to pet her. Then she gave me one dismissive glare and walked away. Her excitement must have overtaken her usual M.O. of being prissy and mercurial. I hoped I would be here long enough to make it up to her.

"Do you want a cup of tea or something?" Abby asked.

"Sure," Luke said. "I'd love to say hi to Ms. Murphy."

"Okay," Abby said. "Just be warned, she's…"

"I won't take up too much of her time."

Abby paused, looking at me. "Mom's upstairs, Jordyn. I'll get Luke his cup of tea and then—"

"That's fine," I said. My heart was pounding in my ears as I realized that I was only moments away from seeing one of my worst nightmares, again.

Someone I love is dying.

Luke looked up at me. "Are you going to be all right?" he asked.

"Yeah," I lied. "I'll be fine."

I plodded up the stairs, each footstep reverberating in my mind. I remembered Mom taking me out to the creek when I was little. I remembered her chasing me on the playground. I remembered everything.

Would those memories go away once she died? Would I forget her face? Those times that made me into the person that I am today?

I didn't know.

As I approached her door, I heard two voices, one of which made me freeze.

"Let me know if you're comfortable, Emma."

Aunt Margaret. Of course she'd be here, taking care of my mother. I wasn't sure if I could face my aunt right now. I hadn't seen her since Zach attacked me in our yard and she determined that the best way to deal with it was my self-imposed exile. I didn't know if the years away had caused her to hate me. Or pity me. Or worse, a combination of both.

"Thanks, Margaret. I don't know what we'd do without you."

My mother sounded weak, ending her statement with a wracking cough. How long had she been feeling ill before she finally went to the doctor? My mother was always particularly tough, especially when she divorced Dad. Once he saw the extent of what being a witch truly meant, he wanted nothing to do with us. She raised us on her own, and she deserved a damn medal for it.

I knocked lightly on the door, interrupting their conversation. I felt the weight in the room, as if they too were wondering what lay beyond the door.

I took a deep breath and opened it.

I didn't know what I expected. I think I imagined my mother to look like a cancer patient with hair loss and a scarf. But she had her hair and there wasn't a scarf to be seen. She only looked like a fragile doll, and in the moment, I realized how beautiful my mother had always been.

Meanwhile, Aunt Margaret looked like she always did too, with her gray hair pulled back into a loose braid down her back, her sea green eyes keen with intelligence. She always dressed in loose, flowing skirts and spaghetti-strap tank tops. While I'd been dreading seeing her, I couldn't help but realize how much I missed her.

On seeing me, my mother's hands flew to her mouth and her eyes filled with tears.

"Jordyn?" she asked weakly.

"*Mom…*"

I went to her side and held her. We rocked each other gently while crying.

"Good to see you, Jordyn," Aunt Margaret said, and she was crying too.

When your family has been splintered and torn apart for any length of time, you realize how much you missed out in life when you're glued back together.

The three of us stayed there, in each other's arms as we cried. It was cathartic. It was liberating. It was something we all needed to do.

After a few minutes, Abby came into the room and crawled into bed with Mom, wrapping her arms around her. This whole ordeal must have been hardest on her. My little sister was a rock star for keeping it all together during this entire ordeal.

We'd been through a lot, and it was unfair that Mom would be going out the way she would. I made a mental note to talk to Aunt Margaret. I had to see if there was anything she could do to stop the progression of Mom's cancer, or cure her entirely. I know I messed up with Zach's spell. I didn't want to risk doing the same thing to Mom, but there had to be something.

I looked up and saw Luke standing idly in the doorway. He must've come up to say 'hi' to Mom, but seeing four of us locked together, he looked unsure if should stay or leave.

"I'll be right back," I said.

I disentangled myself and went to the door, shutting it quietly behind me.

"Sorry about that," I said to him. "We haven't seen each other in a while."

"I know. Sorry for intruding. But I have to report in to work, and I didn't want to leave without saying bye."

"Oh, uhm…"

"I meant saying bye to *you*," Luke corrected, giving me a wry smile.

I raised my eyebrows. "Oh?" I combed a hand through my hair and laughed. "Yes, of course. Sorry, I'm all out of whack right now."

Luke nodded. "I understand."

"Thank you. For picking me up at the airport. I mean, I know that was out of the way for you, and everything."

"It's the least I could do. Considering everything."

I followed him downstairs towards the front door, remembering that I still had to make sure of one thing, a very awkward point with him.

"Hey," I said, "can you do me a favor?"

"Sure."

I tried to pass my request off as a girl who didn't want to confront her ex and not as a former witch who didn't want to aggravate the worst mistake of her life. Because I was both at this point.

"Can you not mention that I'm back in town to your brother? I mean, I'm only here for a bit and I don't—"

"Don't worry about that," Luke answered, his voice rough. "I won't."

I nodded. "Thank you."

"I know this isn't how you wanted to come home," he said, "but I'm glad you're back, Jordyn."

Stupidly, my heart fluttered. "Me too."

There was another awkward pause between us before he nodded distractedly. "Well, I'd better get ready for work."

It took a moment for that to sink in. "Yes, of course," I said, thinking that Christine and the others were probably rehearsing for their performance today. If they had found a replacement for me, that is.

"I'll see you around," Luke said.

"You too."

He looked like he was going to say something else, but he nodded and left.

I closed the door behind him. After a moment's pause, I locked the door, turned the deadbolt, and made sure the curtains were closed. None of those things would stop Zach if he made up his mind to come in, but it certainly put my mind at ease.

"He asks about you, you know."

I looked up the stairs, seeing Abby with her red-rimmed eyes watching me. Her arms crossed over her chest in a protective gesture.

"Who?" I asked Abby dumbly, thinking that she meant Zach.

"Luke."

I frowned. "Oh?"

"For a while, when you were gone, Zach was... scary. Aunt Margaret had to reinforce the protective wards around the house. I wasn't allowed to leave for about a month. Zach stopped by every night, every day, demanding to see you." Abby's voice caught in her throat. "And then, just like Aunt Margaret said, he came over less and less frequently. And then he stopped altogether."

My mistake had terrorized them in my absence. I felt like the lowest of the low. Like I was to blame for everything.

"Luke stops by every so often," Abby continued. "He kept trying to check in on you, to make sure that you were all right. He said that he knew Zach frightened you and wanted to see if you needed help."

"Why didn't anyone tell me that?"

Abby shrugged. "When we told him you had left, he asked us not to."

I wondered why.

"He kept stopping by. Always asked how you were doing. And earlier today, when I didn't want to leave Mom, he volunteered to go." Abby fell silent for a moment. "Sorry about that, by the way. I couldn't…"

"No," I said, shaking my head. "I'm sorry." More tears. I bet a lot of tears were going to fall in the upcoming days. "I left you guys. I left you alone. I'm so sorry, Abby."

My little sister hugged me. "I'm not going to say it's all right and that it's not your fault," she said, her voice clipped and short. "But I do know that you didn't mean the consequences of what you did. In this case, that means just as much."

"I'm so sorry."

"I don't blame you, Jordyn."

That made me cry harder. In a moment of weakness, I put the needs of the few above the needs of others. If I could take it back, I would. If I could have seen the ripples that my resurrecting Zach would have caused, I never would have done it. I think.

"Does Zach know that I'm here?"

Abby pulled back and brushed her tears away with her palms. "No. I've done everything I could to keep it from him."

"He's going to find out though." I felt it in my bones. I felt his presence towering over me, waiting for an opening to come in.

Abby's cheeks flushed again. "I know," she breathed.

"I'll talk to Aunt Margaret about doing an update of

the spells around the house," I decided. "For now though, I want to stay with Mom."

At the very least, I could do that.

CHAPTER 5

I SAT WITH MOM, ABBY, AND AUNT MARGARET for hours, reminiscing about all the good ol' times we had together. At some point, Sadie joined us in the bed, although she slept curled up at the farthest possible corner from us. It was her way of keeping watch over us.

Mom was in good spirits, and I held her hands as we talked until she fell asleep.

"She needs her rest," Aunt Margaret said, ushering us out of the room. "The medicine exhausts her."

"Is there nothing the doctors can do?" I asked.

Aunt Margaret hesitated, then shook her head. "They're investigating some alternative, experimental medicine. But the prognosis isn't good."

I licked my lips, and asked what I really wanted to know. "Is there nothing *you* can do?"

White-faced beside me, Abby shook her head. I'd hit on a nerve.

Aunt Margaret gave me a hard look. "No," she said shortly. She turned on her heel, and headed down the stairs towards the kitchen.

Her answer resounded like depth charges in my

brain. I followed her downstairs and into the kitchen that I was last in three years ago. I practically had to run to keep up with her. Abby called after me, but I ignored her. I was going to get to the bottom of this.

"Why not?" I demanded.

"Why not what?" she asked.

"Why can't you do anything? You're a powerful witch. Mom's not dead—" *yet* "—so we can cure her with something. Boost her immune system up? Banish the disease from her body? *Something?*"

Aunt Margaret whirled on me, her cheeks red with anger. "And then what?" she asked. "We're just going to corrupt her like you did poor Zachary? Turn her into something evil? Something that doesn't resemble anything like the mother you knew?"

"I want to save her," I said tightly. "Surely there has to be a way that doesn't turn into *that.*"

"I know you think you're a powerful witch Jord—"

"*Was* a powerful witch," I corrected. "I haven't practiced anything since then."

Aunt Margaret pursed her lips together. "Then you would have thought you'd have learned your lesson by now. Magick isn't something you can play with."

Her words were like a slap across my cheek. I stiffened my posture. "I simply want to help Mom."

The hardness in her eyes left bit by bit, and my aunt sighed, shaking her head. "Our magick is meant to enhance," she told me. "Purify. Be reflections of ourselves.

It's not meant to manipulate what is *meant to be*."

"So there's nothing we can do?"

"No. And I've been checking, ever since your mother was starting to get sick."

I froze. "How long has she been ill?"

"About a month," Aunt Margaret replied. "First she had a cold that wouldn't go away. They initially thought it was the flu. Then pneumonia. And then they ran a whole bunch of tests. We got the results yesterday, as you know."

"Why didn't anyone tell me she was sick before?" I asked. "Why didn't someone tell me? I would have come back long before now."

Aunt Margaret shook her head. "I don't think anyone wanted to freak you out in case it was nothing."

But it *was* something. Now it was killing my mother, and I could do nothing about it.

I sat down on one of the barstools on the island and put my head in my hands. I rubbed away at the tears. "I just want Mom to be all right."

She rubbed my back. "You're here now," she said gently, her entire demeanor changing. "That's all she wants."

"I didn't want to mess everything up," I cried.

"It *is* messed up," Aunt Margaret said. "What we do now is what determines whether we're good witches or bad witches."

"I don't want to be a witch at all."

Aunt Margaret didn't have an answer for that.

"YOU KNOW WHAT I THINK WE NEED?" AUNT Margaret asked.

It must have been a half hour later. I was still sitting at the island with my head in my hands, having cried my eyes out. Abby had gone up to stay with Mom for a bit, but she left in a hurry not too long ago, claiming that she had to go out with some friends. She seemed different, although after everything that had happened, I wouldn't blame her. Going out would give her a bit of respite from everything. I'm not sure how much of that she'd had lately, so it was good that she was able to act like a normal teenager.

"What?" I asked.

"If I remember correctly," my aunt said, "you used to make a mean chocolate cake."

I snorted a laugh. "Not anymore." After living by myself in Jacksonville and then touring on the road, I hadn't cooked one of those cakes in a long time. It was a recipe that Mom had been using for a long time, like my grandmother before her, and so on. We'd passed it down, much like we passed down our affinity for magick, tweaking little things here and there along the way. When I learned how to make the cake, I'd added my own bit of pizazz by adding cloves to the mix.

"Come on," Aunt Margaret insisted. "Let's bake a cake. For your mom."

I was about to protest, but that addendum to her

statement made me pause. *For Mom.*

It may be a peace offering between my aunt and me, but if it made Mom feel the slightest bit better, it was worth it.

"Okay," I said, allowing a smile to creep onto my face.

Luckily, everything in the kitchen was as I remembered. Pots were in the same place, Mom kept her stockpile of chocolate in the pantry, along with a healthy amount of flour, sugar, and, to my delight, cloves. I hadn't baked much at all in three years, but once I started, muscle memory took over and I got into it.

Aunt Margaret opened a bottle of brandy at one point and started drinking. I actually hadn't had a sip of alcohol since my junior prom, and at twenty, I was still underage, but I took a shot anyway. It burned all the way down and made me feel a little loopy, but it took the edge off. I desperately needed that. In a fit of inspiration, I even decided to add some brandy to the cake mix for something extra. Probably too much brandy, but whatever.

By the time we put the cake in the oven and started prepping the chocolate icing, we were both chatting and laughing, our emotional walls down. Home. Just like I remembered it.

"So tell me," Aunt Margaret said at one point, "what is it like being a mermaid?"

"So. Much. Fun," I said, giggling. Okay, maybe I had two shots of brandy. I stuck a spoon of icing in my mouth, and relished the taste. "Being in the water is amazing."

"Quite a bit different than your Earth-based magick, isn't it? It would suppress it, right?"

"Well, yeah. That's kind of the point of it."

Aunt Margaret grabbed a spoonful of icing herself. "Don't you feel like you're suffocating?"

I asked myself the same question before I took the job at Neptune's World Aquarium. "I was a natural at swimming."

She winked at me. "Maybe you're talented in both Earth *and* Water-based magick."

"I hope not." I picked up the bowl and started stirring harder.

"Why not?"

"Because I've spent the last three years trying *not* to be a witch." I'd been a nursing student, a high school dropout, a mermaid. Anything that wasn't a witch.

"Jordyn…" Aunt Margaret paused to take another shot of brandy, her seventh, I think. "You were born into this family. You're a witch. Always have been. Always will be."

I wanted to respond, but I heard the front door open, and I walked out to see Abby hurriedly padding up the stairs.

"Everything all right?" I asked.

"Peachy keen," Abby said sarcastically.

"Made some cake and—"

The sound of her bedroom door slamming cut off

my words.

I frowned. "What's wrong with Abby?" I asked, looking through to the kitchen.

Aunt Margaret shrugged. "She's seventeen and it's a turbulent time for her. You know what that's like."

Yes, I did know. I saw my boyfriend killed before my eyes, brought him back to life *wrong*, and had to leave the world I knew behind to try and make it right. I messed up. I didn't want Abby following in my footsteps, even if she wasn't a witch. There were plenty of other mistakes you can make as a teenager.

The oven timer beeped, alerting me that the cake was done. I went back into the kitchen, making a mental note to talk to Abby later, and possibly cheer everyone up with a piece of cake, even though a cake wouldn't make everything better.

***

THANKFULLY, I HADN'T LOST MY TOUCH AT baking. The cake turned out moist and delicious, made even more decadent with the addition of brandy. I'd include it in the recipe when I baked again.

Mom was in better spirits when she woke up, and Abby didn't address her weird mood when she came back. She didn't explain, and I didn't ask although she acted indifferent.

We ordered a pizza for dinner, sat around Mom's

bed, and talked, catching up. Sure, I Skyped and called them frequently, but nothing compared with reconnecting face-to-face.

I missed this.

Though Aunt Margaret only lived a few houses down, she retired to the guest room, saying that she wasn't going to leave for even a second while Mom was sick. My room was the same, even down to the One Direction posters on the walls. Those were the first things I took down, as well as a few other things that reminded me too much of time that I'd never get back.

Sometime after midnight, I finally laid down. I'd checked my emails on my phone and texted everyone about today's events, both of which took longer than I expected. After my red eye flight to Jacksonville, I was exhausted, so it didn't take long for me to fall asleep.

***

TAP.

Tap.

Tap.

My eyes snapped open at the noise on my window. Cold dread filled me, making it hard to breathe. *No.*

Tap.

Tap.

I could ignore it. Hope that it wasn't him. If it *was* him, I could hope that he'd give up and go home. Except, deep down I knew that he wouldn't, not until I spoke with him. Until then, he was going to keep it up, and it was only going to get more insistent until he got a response.

Tap.

My decision was made. I wrapped my comforter around me and went to the dormer window. I held my breath as I parted the curtains and looked down.

At first, I didn't see anything. The backyard to my mom's house is small, with a wall of flowers separating it from Mr. Samson's yard. But then, another pebble hit the glass, making me shriek. Then I saw movement below.

Disheveled dark hair. Dull, blue eyes.

Zachary Harington looking up at me. Expecting me. Waiting for me.

I unlatched the window and opened it.

"Thought I smelled something familiar here," he said, his lips spreading into a ghastly grin. Even in the moonlight, he didn't look like the Zach I knew. He looked like someone had made a paper mask and pasted it over his face. His eyes were too small for the sockets, and his smile was too wide with teeth too small for their spaces.

I covered my mouth, stifling a sob.

What has happened to him? Did I do this?

"Zach?"

"Yes, Love?" he snarled up at me, that creepy grin remaining. "Or wait. I was mistaken in that." He took a step towards me. "I should call you 'Slut'. Or 'Homewrecker'. Or even 'Devil Spawn'. You *are* a witch, after all."

"Look, Zach. I'm sorry."

He shook his head. "Sorry doesn't cut it. Sorry implies forgiveness, which you don't deserve. No. *You left me!*" he yelled, his voice ringing out in the night. Birds took off from their perches in the trees, disturbed by his rant. I wished I could fly away, too.

He stopped as soon as he heard his own voice echo back to him, threw back his head, and laughed. "You're frightened of me, aren't you?"

"Yes."

He craned his neck back to look at me. "Why?" He took in a gasping sob. "When all I have ever done is *love you*?"

"I wronged you, Zach." My voice was soft, but I knew he could hear me. "I just didn't want to let you go."

"You never *had* to let me go!" he shouted. "*You* were the one who left."

I shook my head. "That's not what I meant. You know that."

"What do I know?" He took a few more steps, almost directly below me. He was looking straight up at me, his lips curled up into a sneer. "Only that I was left alone. No choices. No hope for the future. You have to help me. I'm so lost. So lost without you. Why am I like this? *Why?*"

"Zachary, you need to go home."

"No!" he shouted. He started pacing, shaking his head wildly. "No, you don't get to send me away like that! You don't have that right anymore, Jordyn! *Jordyn!*"

He took a running start and leapt towards the window, impossibly high. I don't know whether it was because I was home or if it was because my senses were heightened at that moment and I was more attuned to Earth, but the spell formed easily in my mind, despite the fact that I'd been fighting magick for three years now. A banishment spell.

I shouted it as his hands hit the windowsill, scrabbling for purchase. The blast hit him in the face, knocking him backwards into the bushes tucked out of sight below me.

"Jordyn?" I glanced behind me to see my great aunt in the doorway. She looked at me, her expression shrewd. "What's happening? Is he here?"

In the split second it took for me to look down, I saw that Zach was barreling off into the flower bushes beyond our property, through Mr. Samson's backyard and beyond.

I collapsed to the floor, sobbing.

I shouldn't have come home. Otherwise, Zach would still be all right. And no one else would be hurt.

I'm so sorry, Zach.

Throughout all of this, he was the one I failed the most.

CHAPTER 6

THAT NIGHT, MY DREAMS WERE FILLED WITH nightmarish images of Zach chasing me through Shady Point on a dark, starless night. I was wearing my prom dress and running as fast as I could away from the monster I accidentally created.

Lights flashed through the trees, the same bright white-yellow color at the same height with the same engine noises that I remember from that car. The lights turned towards me, and I froze, unable to move.

The car careened towards me, and I was transfixed with fear.

The impact that shoved me aside didn't come from steel and chrome. Zach pushed me out of the way at the last second, saving me from the car-monster. It struck him, once again throwing his body over the hood, rolling it brokenly before it landed on the ground and the car disappeared into the night.

Despite the fact that I had just been running from him, I couldn't ignore the fact that someone I once loved—someone that I still cared about—lay dying.

I ran to his side to see the bloody, tangled mess that

he now was.

Only his face wasn't Zach's.

It was Luke's.

***

THE DOORBELL WOKE ME THE NEXT MORNING. I sat up with a jolt, not knowing where I was. It was amazing that I had slept in this bed for most of my life, yet it felt so unfamiliar.

I pulled on a pair of yoga pants and peeked around the door. From my vantage point on the second floor landing, I saw that Aunt Margaret had answered the door.

Two police officers were at the front door, one of them Luke. They spoke in low voices with Aunt Margaret, who went from looking confused to utterly horrified.

"No," she said. "No, that isn't possible."

Luke's eyes flicked up to the second floor landing, meeting mine. "Jordyn?"

I gulped down some air and made my way down the stairs and to the front door.

"Yes?" I managed, my heart in my throat.

Luke looked like he was about to ask a question, then his partner stepped in. He was an older cop who looked like he pumped too much iron yet didn't lay off the donuts. His name badge said that he was Officer Pratt, and I could already tell that he had a bias against my family. After living with it for seventeen years, I could tell by his expression that he was about ready to accuse me of witchcraft.

"Where were you between the hours of three and five this morning?" he demanded without preamble.

"Umm…"

I tried remembering what time I saw Zach last night. I'd been so traumatized by the entire ordeal, I hadn't thought about doing a mental time stamp of last night's events. "I was asleep. Here."

Luke was frowning at me, not unkindly, but unhappily. *What's going on?*

Pratt pounded on it though. "Do you have anyone who can vouch for your whereabouts?"

I was glad that Luke was here. I had the feeling that if Officer Pratt was by himself, we'd all be burned on a cross.

"I can," Aunt Margaret said. "We had a disturbance, so I was in her room around that time." She looked to me for my reaction, but I was still too shocked to really process anything.

"What kind of disturbance?" Luke asked, stepping in.

"We had an unwelcome intruder that wanted to talk to Jordyn," Aunt Margaret continued. "Your brother stopped by."

Luke visibly paled. "About what time?"

"About two thirty," Aunt Margaret answered. "Placing Jordyn here. And since she doesn't have a vehicle, it makes it hard to put her anywhere near the crime scene, right?"

"Crime scene?" I repeated. Nothing was making any sense.

"Do you know David Posey or Shea Blaine?" Officer Pratt asked.

The names sounded familiar, and took a moment for me to place where I'd heard them before. "Oh, they were students...at my high school. The year before me."

Pratt leaned into me, smelling of cigarettes and sweat. "They were found dead last night. At Shady Point."

The same place where Zach was killed.

"They had apparently gone there for a lover's rendezvous," the police officer said. "We found them this morning."

"Killed?" I asked, shocked.

Pratt apparently took this as me admitting guilt. "What do you know about it?" he demanded, pushing his way into the foyer.

"Nothing!" I exclaimed, taken aback by his roughness.

"Chuck," Luke warned, stepping in between us, although his face was pale from fear.

Officer Pratt huffed. "Miss Murphy, your jacket was found at the scene."

As if in protest, my hands flew to my hips to see if my jacket was there. It wasn't. I hadn't seen it since sometime yesterday. Where the hell was it? I shook my head. "My jacket was at the scene?"

Officer Pratt nodded. "Why would your jacket be at the scene, Miss Murphy?"

"I have no idea," I said. "I got here yesterday because my mom is…" My stomach lurched. "How'd you know it was my jacket?"

"You left your license in the pocket," Officer Pratt snarled.

I must have tucked in there when I went through security at LAX. I was so paranoid at the prospect of flying, I'd completely forgotten to put it back in my purse.

"Plus, Luke remembers you wearing that jacket yesterday."

Luke scratched his head, uneasy about being called out. Anger swelled up inside me that he would immediately identify my jacket. Actually…

"I took my jacket off in your car," I said, glancing Luke. "When I came got home yesterday."

He shook his head. "It wasn't there when I got back."

"But…"

Our eyes connected and I knew that he could guess my next thought.

"I was on duty all night," he said.

So he had an alibi. At least that's what it sounded like.

"Can you come down to the station and make a statement?" he asked gently. He looked at Aunt Margaret. "You too, Miss Margaret, since you're her alibi."

"Let me grab my purse," she said, turning away.

"Are you arresting me?" I asked.

"No," Luke said.

"Not yet," Pratt added ominously, giving the younger

man a dirty look.

My mind raced at a million miles a second, thinking back to last night. After Zach left my house, did he go to Shady Point where he killed two people in a fit of rage? And brought my jacket with him? From Luke's car? It didn't make any sense.

Luke made eye contact with me, a question in his gaze. I kept my mouth shut. After all, didn't my Miranda Rights state that anything I said could and would be used against me? In Centerburg, I knew that people would try to twist my words around.

"I'm ready," Aunt Margaret said, wrapped up in her coat.

Officer Pratt gave me wide berth when I walked by him. Crazily, I thought about faking him out threateningly, but that probably wouldn't help my case. Besides, I was wondering *how* this could have happened. I'd done nothing wrong. At least in regards to killing anyone.

I'd done plenty wrong otherwise.

***

"WELL, THAT'S AN INTERESTING WAY TO SPEND a Monday morning," my great aunt declared as we re-entered the house. She gave me a stern look and went into the kitchen. It was two hours later, near lunchtime, and I was sure she'd rather be cooking than talking to me about happened.

What exactly *did* happen?

When they took us to the station, they separated us to see if our stories matched. Officer Pratt asked me a bunch of questions about last night, questions that I didn't have answers to. I told him as much as I could, though it didn't appease him. When I wrote down my statement, detailing everything I could remember last night, I included the part about Zach appearing in the backyard, hoping it would lend credibility to my story.

It didn't.

When Officer Pratt had a look at my statement, to "make sure it was correct", he got angry and left the room for a bit. When he came back, he said that I was free to go but warned me not to leave town in case they wanted to ask me more questions.

I wasn't leaving, even if it impacted Zach. I had made up my mind that I wasn't going to let him terrorize me. I was going to do something about it.

I wasn't going to be frightened of him anymore, and he wasn't going to hurt anyone else.

The entire time we were at the station, Luke was nowhere to be seen. It would have been good to have a friend in my corner during all this, especially since he had identified the coat as mine. The next time I saw him I was going to tell him how pissed I was that he left us hanging in the wind

Officer Pratt drove Aunt Margaret and me back to the house. He didn't say a single word the entire time, which was fine by me. It gave me time to replay yesterday's events. I knew that I left the jacket in Luke's car when I got out to hug Abby. That meant that Zach must have driven Luke's car or grabbed the jacket when he went to Shady Point.

Either that or Luke did it.

I felt sick at that thought. What if it *was* Luke?

I didn't get any other information about David and Shea's deaths. So many questions floated around my head, mainly *why?*

Now, standing in the foyer in my old house, I had to figure out what happened even if that meant opening up those floodgates to the one person that I tried to leave behind.

Sadie meowed me at me, stalking her way towards me. She rubbed herself against my calves, marking me as hers.

"Hey girl," I said, bending down to give her a pat. She didn't like that, so she trotted away from me in that pissed off way that cats have. I sighed.

I hurried up the stairs and gently knocked on Mom's door. When I opened it, I saw Abby curled up next to her. They were both asleep, and Abby's brown hair was swirled around the two of them.

I never realized how much the two of them looked alike. I wondered how much of Mom was reflected in me. How much of me was a witch like her.

I'd spent three years trying to suppress that side of

me. And here I was, wanting to dabble in it again, this time to bind Zach, or do something to make his after life as normal as it could be. Though I might not be able to completely make things right, there had to be something I could do.

"Mom?"

Abby stirred first. Her brown eyes opened, spearing me with an unhappy expression, telling me to get lost.

"What, honey?" my mom rasped. She was awake now.

"Can we talk?"

"Of course, Jordyn."

"About what we can do with Zach."

Abby flinched and rolled away from my mother. She gave me a dirty look as she stalked past me, out of Mom's room. She bumped into me as she passed, knocking me off balance.

"Leave her be," Mom said, her voice sounding even more ragged now.

"What's her problem?"

Mom sighed. "She's just being a moody teenager. This has been hard on her."

Me, too.

"Jordyn," Mom said gently, "about Zach, he—"

"There has to be something we can do," I said. "He came here last night."

Mom lay back on her pillow, closing her eyes. "He was bound to find out that you were here, honey," she cut in. "He'll be back to normal once you're gone again."

Once you're gone again. I recoiled at that. "I don't think he was ever normal though, Mom."

I felt like I was being dismissed. Not only that, but based on what Luke said, Zach certainly had never gone back to normal. He'd been tormented, changed by what I'd done to him. This wasn't normal. And if my suspicions were right, then…

"I think he killed some people last night."

My mother sucked in a deep breath and pushed herself up in her bed with the little strength she had left. "What?"

"Aunt Margaret and I just got back from the police station. Two people were killed at the same place where he died earlier. *After* he visited me last night."

Mom managed to pale further, then her eyes flicked to someone behind me.

"Margaret…"

"Don't worry about this morning, Emma." My great aunt stepped into the room. She gave me a cross look before striding into the room. "We made our statements to the police."

"Until they try charging me," I muttered.

"Charging you?" my mother exclaimed.

"That won't happen," Aunt Margaret said, assuring her more than me.

"Bullshit," I said, thinking about Officer Pratt who clearly had it out for me. "Mom, they found my jacket at the crime scene."

"What else did they find?"

I shook my head. "I don't know."

"That's because they have nothing to charge us with," Aunt Margaret said evenly.

"You think Zachary did it?" Mom asked me.

"He had to," I said. "I mean, it's too big to be a coincidence, right?"

"I don't know," Aunt Margaret admitted.

"Is there *any way* we can bind him?" I pleaded. "To make him be a good person again? Like he was before?"

My mother and Aunt Margaret exchanged glances, not answering my question.

That was all the answer I needed. So there *was* a way. They didn't even have to investigate or search for the right spell. I thought it had been a long shot, or some sort of project, but no. They *knew* of one.

The truth slapped me harder than any of the name calling that I had grown up with. They knew about a spell for Zach, yet they hadn't cast it. Instead, I'd been forced to move away from the only life I knew, thinking that there had been an unsolvable problem in the form of Zach Harington.

Angry tears sprang into my eyes. "There is one. And you've been keeping it from me."

"Jordyn—" my mom started.

"It's not what it appears to be," Aunt Margaret said.

My hands clenched at my sides. I needed jump

into a pool or some other body of water. I needed to be surrounded by another element because I was about to tap into that earth-based magick that I'd spent three years trying to clamp down on. Where was a swimming pool when I needed it?

"It appears to be a lot of things," I said.

"Jordyn, honey," Mom said. The hurt in her own voice gave me pause. She patted the bed. "Please come here."

Anger didn't suit me very well, leaving me drained. I sighed and sat at the foot of the bed. Out of reach, but still close enough.

"We've already tried a binding spell," Aunt Margaret said.

"What? When?"

"Before you left," Mom said.

My mind whirled about *when* that could have happened. Then the pieces fit into place. When they had locked themselves up in the library, they had tried everything. They must have tried a spell that they were sure would have helped Zach, but it failed miserably. Especially for them to not mention it to me.

"Then why—"

"The magick surrounding Zach," Aunt Margaret said, "the magick that is keeping him alive—it's too strong and too dark for us to fully have control over his tendencies." She sighed. "We're able to maintain some semblance of him being bound, but it's not without its price."

"A price?" I echoed, feeling my heart turning to ice at those words. Nothing in magick is ever one-sided. Like Newton's Law, for every action, there was an opposite reaction. Only, with witchcraft, it came back three times stronger.

"Mom, is your cancer…?" My voice caught in my throat. I couldn't even get the words out. "Is that the price?"

Mom hesitated to answer.

I sprang up like there was a snake under my feet. "How long? How long have you known that this was going to happen?"

"I knew there was always a risk," Mom said. "It was worth it. For you."

"No. No it's not." Tears flooded my eyes. "Mom, I—"

"Jordyn," Aunt Margaret said, "your mother did this so that Zach wouldn't follow you out of Centerburg. So that you could live a normal life."

Exactly what I didn't want to hear. My mother had sacrificed everything for me.

Conflicting emotions warred within me. I turned on my heel and fled to my room, where I had spent so much of my childhood. Where I had spent countless hours on the phone with Zach. Where I had laid the foundations for my family's deterioration.

I collapsed on the bed, crying until it felt like I dried up the deep well of emotion deep inside me.

I had ruined everything for both my family and Zach's, and now Mom was paying the price. Not only that, but I had no idea what would happen once she was gone. If they were binding Zach with her life force, would he then start following me everywhere once she was gone? Would he get worse?

I was responsible for this.

And there was nothing worse than that realization.

***

SOMETIME LATER, THERE WAS A KNOCK ON my door. I didn't respond have time to repsond before my little sister barged in.

She crossed her arms and leaned against the door, regarding me with her hard expression. "Now you know," she said simply.

"You knew?"

She fretted with her split ends. "Mom only told me yesterday. When I went up upstairs while you were being a baby in the kitchen." Abby pushed off the door and sat in my old computer chair, facing me. "She talks in her sleep, you know. Especially when they have her on strong medication."

"I didn't know."

"She must have had some pretty bad nightmares because she mentioned the binding spell. When she woke up, I asked her about it. And she told me everything." She shook her head. "Talk about dropping a bombshell."

So that was why Abby's entire demeanor had changed yesterday. "I never knew."

"Yeah, well," Abby said, casting her eyes down.

"I'm so sorry."

Abby didn't give me platitudes by saying that it was all right or that I was young when I did it. That wasn't what would help now. What would help was trying to find another way.

I could help her. I'd been holding back my magick for years, but I would fall back into it if it meant my mother could live longer.

"We could save her."

Abby gave me a suspicious look. "Don't you think you've done enough damage, Jordyn?"

That stung, but I wasn't about to let it go. Not when my mother's life was on the line. Call me stupid—after all, I'd dabbled in trying to save lives before—but this was different. This was trying to atone for my past mistakes.

"I mean we find another way to stop Zach. Take the burden off Mom."

Abby shook her head. "No, absolutely not."

"We could look in spell books. We could—"

"*Jordyn!*" my sister exclaimed, exasperated. "Please. Drop it." She got to her feet and stormed out of the room.

"Abby," I pleaded, following her out. She disappeared into her own room just as the doorbell rang.

Ugh, what now?

What if it was Zach again? I couldn't handle him right now. Especially if he had killed David and Shea but I didn't want the doorbell to disturb Mom.

I padded down the stairs to the front door. Luckily, it had a peephole. I steadied myself, working to calm my rapidly beating heart before I dared to look. I stood up on my tiptoes and peered through, holding my breath.

It was Luke in plainclothes meaning that he wasn't here on official police business. My anger from earlier reared its ugly head, remembering that he practically fed me to the wolves this morning.

With shaking hands, I undid the locks and opened it.

He pushed past me, inside the house, thankfully allowing me enough room to close the door. Maybe Zach wasn't loitering around. That also was a scary idea, because I didn't want to think about where he could be.

"Are you all right, Jordyn?" Luke asked.

No. I choked back all of the recent revelations and focused on the bone that I did have to pick with him.

"Where were you?" I asked, crossing my arms. "I mean, you took us to the station, and then you disappeared. Your buddy Chris Pratt has it out for me and—"

"His name is actually Chuck," he quietly corrected. "And yes, he's an asshole."

I stared at him, bewildered. "Where the hell were you?"

"They wouldn't let me see you. They said it would be a conflict of interest if I was there to take your statement."

He combed both of his hands through his hair, something that I recognized as a nervous habit.

I frowned. "It sucked."

"Did you do it?"

"What?" Did he actually think I would kill someone?

"Did you kill David and Shea?"

I stared at him, aghast. "*No!*"

"Your jacket was found at the scene."

"That doesn't mean that I was there!"

"It's pretty convincing evidence."

"Do you think that if I was going to kill someone, I'd leave my jacket on the scene? That would be pretty stupid of me."

Luke leveled me with his gaze. "It *would* be pretty stupid." He wasn't agreeing with me; he was accusing me.

"You think I did that? I left my jacket in your car. For all I know, *you* did it."

As soon as it left my lips, I felt guilty for pointing the finger back at him.

He actually laughed at that. "I didn't murder them."

"Neither did I."

He groaned and combed his hands through his hair more. "You're not making this any easier."

"I didn't do it, Luke," I insisted.

I could have told him that I thought it was Zach, but what good would that do? Luke already thought I did it. My condemnation of his younger brother would only serve to make my case worse. Plus, I honestly didn't know if it was Zach, even if it made the most sense.

"I don't know."

Luke deflated. "Look, Jordyn—"

"Don't come barging in here, accusing me of doing something I didn't do. Isn't that against the rules? Or the law? Or something?"

He was quiet for a second before he answered. "I believe you."

I glared at him and he shrank under my gaze, reminding me of everyone who always accused me of hexing them.

"Are you done?" I asked, tired.

His cheeks reddened. "I guess. I had to hear it from you. That you didn't do it. I didn't want my feelings to get in the way."

I put my hands on my hips. "Your feelings?" I intoned. "Luke, we're friends. You should know that I could never, would never, do that. I screw things up by saving lives, not taking them."

"No, Jordyn, I mean—Agh! This is so hard. I mean, I like-like you." He gave me a meaningful look.

"What?"

It actually took a full minute for that to sink in. Then I remembered that Abby had told me that he still asked about me and the pieces clicked into place. My own cheeks burned bright red.

"*Oh.*"

"Yeah," he said sheepishly.

Suddenly everything made a whole lot more sense. My heart pounded in my ears, this time for a different reason. Luke Harington liked me. Luke, the older brother of my only boyfriend. Whose life I ruined. Both of their lives I ruined.

Not only that, but it was Luke, the same boy who saw me run around naked in our front yards when I was three. Luke, who sometimes picked me up after middle school because no one else wanted to offer the witch a ride home when it rained too hard.

"How long?" I asked, my voice strangled.

"A long time." He laughed mirthlessly. "A very long time."

I searched his face, trying to see if he would crack a smile and tell me that it was all a joke. He would do that, right?

However, he only looked at me with this earnest expression, hoping for some sort of reciprocity from me. And this, well, this blindsided me.

How had he been able to keep it a secret all our lives? How horrible was it to see his younger brother date me and to see me break his heart?

"Listen," Luke said hurriedly, my shocked silence making him uncomfortable, "if you said you didn't do it, I believe you."

I frowned, feeling my heart break at his predicament. "If me saying that I didn't do it sways your decision, then your feelings *are* getting in the way."

"Yeah. I guess so. I guess that doesn't make me a very good policeman. But…"

"I promise I didn't do it," I said.

The silence between us stretched out uncomfortably. Finally, he coughed, and his business exterior slipped back into place. "All right, then." He looked at my lips, and I could see the indecision there, about whether or not he was going to try to make a move. He turned away.

Why was my heart fluttering?

"See you later, Jordyn."

"Bye, Luke."

I closed the door behind him and pressed my forehead to it. This was something you'd find on daytime television. *The older brother of my ex-boyfriend likes me, while the ex in question is trying to kill me.*

Yep. Soap opera material.

I needed to find a way to remove the binding on Zach so it wouldn't kill my mother, and then find another alternative for Zach, all while trying to keep him from killing others.

It sounded easy. Not.

CHAPTER 7

"JORDYN, WHAT ARE YOU DOING?" ABBY groaned.

Sitting on the floor with piles of old *Books of Shadows* and spell books surrounding me, I flipped through the pages of one, frowning.

"Looking for a binding spell," I answered simply.

I was in the library where Mom and Aunt Margaret spent several days three years ago. My family had been witches for centuries, and some of my ancestors were incredibly powerful. Surely, I'd find something. Even with the age of some of the books, I felt the immense power inside them.

Why are you doing this?" Abby asked.

I closed the book with a snap. "I want to find a way to remove the spell that's on Zach to save Mom. Then I need to find something else to bind him with. Or banish him." There was always that, but we had no idea what he would do if we weren't nearby.

Abby shook her head and I could see that she was crying. "Both Mom and Aunt Margaret did this three years ago, and look what happened. Mom did something that cursed her. And now *you* want to do that?"

"Maybe they weren't looking in the right place."

"I thought you gave up witchcraft!" Abby exclaimed. "You said that you wouldn't do any of this stuff again! And here you are looking for—"

"For Mom, I'll do anything. Wouldn't you?"

"Yes. Not like this though."

"I've made mistakes in the past. I'm not going to do anything to risk her or our family ever again."

"Jordyn…" Abby's eyes filled with tears, "please don't turn her into Zach."

Before I could assure her that I only wanted to bind Zach and not bring Mom back from the dead, she turned on her heel and left, slamming the library door behind her. I winced at the loud noise.

It was a warped sense of what was wrong and what was right. But I *knew* I had to do this. I had to save Mom. Or else…

I pushed those horrible thoughts from my mind and picked up the next book, flipping through the handwritten pages and diagrams, though my quick, cursory glances came up with nothing.

I set that book aside and moved onto the next one and the next until the unread pile became smaller than the read pile, and I was running out of options. Surely—*surely* there was something in here that we could use.

Luckily, no one else came into the library while I was there. I could only imagine how angry Aunt Margaret would have been to see me here.

After I'd combed through all the books, I sat back on my heels, angry tears sliding down my cheeks. I had found nothing that was strong enough to do the trick. From what I'd read, the magick that I had plucked out of thin air to revive Zach was wicked strong and borne out of my desperation to save him. You would have thought there'd be something that could save Mom in similar circumstances, but I had to be in the same frame of mind.

I wish there was someone else I could ask.

Aunt Margaret certainly wasn't going to help, and if she couldn't find anything here, then there wasn't really anything else I could ask her for. Mom wasn't in any condition for me to pester her, and there wasn't anyone else near us.

Unless…

The thought was crazy, but as I entertained the idea, it became less and less so. While searching, I'd come across a few different spells for communicating with spirits to find answers to problems. I pulled one of the books out from the pile. It was from my great-great-great grandmother who I learned from flipping through her book was a spiritual medium. Her book wasn't effective if I was looking for a spell for binding and banishment, but as one for communicating with spirits, it was perfect.

I'd ask one of my ancestors for help. And if that didn't work then…

I'm not going there. Not yet.

I flipped through some pages, landing on a spell. After a cursory glance, I believed that I had everything I needed at the house, except a full moon. The blood moon was two nights ago, when I received the news that Mom was sick. I did the math in my head. I should be good to do it tonight. It would be full enough, I hoped.

The worst part was I'd have to be outside, which put me at risk of Zach sniffing me out, and I decided it was a risk I'd have to take. I'd have to do it late tonight, when everyone was in bed, or else they'd try to stop me.

I shut the heavy book with a thud and got to my feet, bringing it with me. I had some planning to do.

***

"OKAY, THAT SHOULD BE IT."

I set down the canister of salt, put my hands on my hips, and inspected my handiwork. This was my first spell in three years, so I was shaking a bit. I stood in the middle of a circle of salt that meant to protect me from Zach and any other evil entities that might be lurking about. Most witches agree that spells are more powerful when the person casting them fully believes in them, however, I felt apprehensive, which made it a self-perpetuating prophecy.

I should hurry and minimize the risk of alerting Zach.

It took way too long for night to fall and even longer for everyone to go to bed. After I gathered all of the things

I needed for the communication spell, I'd stayed with Mom. Luckily, Abby didn't rat me out, so I didn't have to defend my actions. Whether it was because of a sister's code or what, I was thankful that she didn't spill the beans, though she did give me a suspicious look.

Hopefully this would solve all of our problems and she could forgive me later.

I knelt and looked at the book, which was open to the spell in question. I lit five white candles in a circle around me and cleared my mind. I knew that the next part was going to be tricky. I didn't know who I was summoning, except that I wanted someone who could answer my questions. The spell specifically asked me to write the name of the spirit on a piece of paper and imagine what they looked like.

Here's hoping that I was still the gifted witch that my mother and Aunt Margaret said I was. My rustiness pulled at the edges of my mind, taunting me. I took out a slip of parchment paper and wrote, *Spirit*, while imagining not what they looked like, but imagined what they might know. Hopefully that was enough, and I wasn't going to call up a demon or something. That would be the cherry on top.

I passed the slip of paper through the flame of the candle in front of me, reciting the spell:

"Shadows lurking in the night,

I summon you,

Come to me tonight."

I said it two more times, imbuing as much of my

energy into those words as possible, so much that it created an instant headache. Hopefully that meant that I was doing everything possible. A cold wind picked up, bringing with it a scent of earthy moss and wet dirt.

I inhaled, letting it fill up my senses. It brought me home, aligned me with my element of Earth. I'd been so disconnected from this part of myself for too long. It felt like an old friend was welcoming me back into the fold.

Then I felt it, the presence of spirits surrounding my circle of protection, whispering on the corners of my mind. The spirits hadn't fully materialized yet, so I couldn't see who they were. Apparently, in asking for someone who could help, I had summoned far more than one spirit.

That was okay though. My odds that one of them could help were higher with more spirits.

This was going to work.

"Hey, Love."

I whirled at the voice. *No, no, no.*

"Zach?" I called out into the darkness. My heart pounded in my ears as I strained to listen to the night air.

There was nothing. Maybe I had imagined it after all.

"*Jordyn.*"

The voice came from right next to me. I screeched and backed up to the opposite end of my circle of salt. Zach stood on the edge, watching me with that horrible expression that he had last night. Up close, he looked like a decaying clown.

Thankfully though, the circle of protection was

working—he hadn't stepped inside the ring of salt yet.

"What are you doing here?"

He cocked his head, watching me with those dead, mossy eyes. "What am I doing here?" he echoed. "You called me."

"What do you mean?"

"I heard you. Calling for me."

Calling for him. I covered my mouth to bite back an angry curse. *Stupid, stupid, stupid, Jordyn.*

In summoning a nonspecific spirit, I had called him too. "You don't need to be here, Zach," I said, swallowing uncomfortably.

"You wanted someone who could help you," he said, taking one menacing step closer to me.

I nodded, trying to appease him, but then I began furiously shaking my head. "Yes, but—"

"Who knows a better way to get rid of me," he said, quirking a creepy smile, "than *me*?"

His words sunk in. First came the horror and the worry about what he'd do since he heard that part of my summoning. Then came the wonder about *what if?* What if he really *did* know how to cure himself?

What if the answer to all our problems this entire time had been *him?* And not only binding him or banishing him—what if he knew something that would help?

"Can you help me, Zach?"

"Yes."

"How?"

He moved forward until the tips of his shoes were millimeters from the circle of salt. Those eyes that reminded me of a shark's watched me keenly, a slow smile creeping across his lips. "I want to be put to rest. Forever this time."

"So you want me to kill you?"

Admittedly, it wasn't the first time that I'd thought of that option, but every time, I remembered Aunt Margaret telling me that I couldn't right a wrong with another wrong. It wasn't my place to kill him, like it wasn't my place to bring him back.

Zach violently shook his head. "No, no, no, no, no, no. *No!*"

"How do I put you to rest?"

With a loud crack as if he'd popped all the vertebrae in his neck at once, the violent shaking stopped, Zach's head completely to the side in profile. The eye rolled in his socket and he looked at me. "Find who killed me."

I still felt uneasy, but it made sense in some sort of twisted way. "Then what?"

His creepy smile faded and he stilled. "I'll have justice."

"And you won't hurt me?"

"I never wanted to hurt—"

"You choked me Zach. If I wasn't wearing a protection charm then, I could have died."

He knelt by the circle and pressed himself up to the ward as close as possible. "It's just...sometimes you get stuck up here." He beat at his head, like he was trying to knock some water out of his ears. "You get stuck and I. Can't. Get. You. Out."

The cadence of his voice made my stomach twist in sympathy. He sounded like a lost, wild animal trying to fit in. Except, as a dead man walking, Zach wasn't going to fit in anywhere.

"I'm sorry," I said.

"I need to get rid of *you*. So I can get rid of *me*."

I thought about it, still not really believing that I actually was considering this whole thing. There was still one more question I had to ask. "Why did you kill David and Shea last night?"

The air suddenly changed with my question, and Zach's entire demeanor transformed. It was as if a demon clawed its way back into his mind, taking over again. The sad, inept Zach that was here before was gone.

"I didn't kill them!" he snarled. "If you loved me, you bitch, you wouldn't think I did it!"

I got to my feet, meaning to comfort him, but he matched my height, and I remembered once again how much taller my football-playing ex-boyfriend was than me. "Okay! Zach!"

"I didn't kill them!" He began pounding on the shield that the circle created for me. Every time his fit hit the invisible barrier, I could see it crack like glass. It wasn't going to hold up if this continued any longer. "You're pathetic! You still can't put two and two together!

You don't think that someone who would have run over a teenager wouldn't do the same thing three years later? Use your brain." He turned to leave. "Use that damn brain, Jordyn. I swear. You want a place to start, look there."

He dissolved into the night, as if he was a shadow melting into the darkness.

I stared at the space where he left, trying to get my heartbeat under control. If he was lying and he was the one that had killed the couple last night, I wondered if he was going to do it again.

A piece of me believed him, however, it was a weird coincidence that when I asked for spirits for help, *he* was the one who showed up to help. Almost like he was a ghost haunting himself.

I blew out the candles, going counterclockwise from north to close the circle. Then I grabbed my things and moved aside a section of salt, opening the ward. I sprinted back to the house in case Zach decided to return.

I reached the back porch without incident, breathing heavier than I should have been. I was rocked to my core by this entire thing. I opened the sliding door and stepped inside.

"So you *did* do something stupid."

I started at the voice and flipped the lights on. "Abby?"

My sister had been sitting at the island in the dark, watching me through the glass. Even in the dark, I could tell that her expression wasn't happy, but it wasn't mad either. It was like she was resigned to this fact that her sister was going to dabble in things she shouldn't.

"I told you not to do anything stupid, Jordyn," she groaned

"I can get rid of Zach," I told her quickly.

She rolled her eyes, not believing me. "Was that why he was shouting at you?"

"Kinda."

"Why would he want you to get rid of him?"

"I don't think he wants to be here either."

"Well, that's not news. No one wants to be stuck in Centerburg."

Despite myself, I laughed at her comment. She had a very different view of the town we grew up in than I. She had wanderlust, while all I wanted was to be able to return home with every fiber of my being. Funny how you want what you can't have.

Maybe after this, I can finally have what I want.

"He wants me to find the person who killed him, and then he can be at peace."

"He thinks the person who killed him—" she blanched at using those words, "—the person who *hit* him is still around?"

"Apparently so. And he thinks they killed David and Shea."

"But why haven't the cops been able to find who did it? If the person who killed him was nearby, wouldn't they have been arrested?"

"I don't know." I chewed at my bottom lip. "Can you do me a favor?"

"What?" She didn't sound enthused.

"Can you drive me out to Shady Point?"

Abby paled. "What, to check out the crime scene?"

"Well, that. But to also revisit where he was hit. See if there's anything we missed."

"Don't you think that would be suspicious if you were caught?"

I hadn't thought about that. "I need to go, Abby. I won't get caught." I'd see if there was a charm here that could conceal us if need be.

"Okay. Tomorrow?"

"No," I said. "Tonight. *Please.*"

After all, there wasn't a blood moon, so someone I cared about wasn't going to die. However, I was worried about others dying if I didn't try to stop it tonight. Zach was agitated when he left and there was no telling what he'd do.

Abby gave me a hard look, then sighed. "Fine."

CHAPTER 8

EVEN THOUGH SHADY POINT HAD BEEN A murder scene less than twenty-four hours ago, it was eerily easy to get behind the yellow crime scene tape. I looked around in the dark, ghostly memories haunting me. Even though it was ludicrous, I swore that all of the trees looked the same as they did that fateful night.

The nearly full moon illuminated the area so much, it almost wasn't necessary to use a flashlight. I wouldn't have used one, except for the fact that I was terrified. My hands shook and I took a deep breath to steady them.

Abby wasn't happy about driving thirty minutes outside of town at two in the morning or joining me in this dark, spooky place. She clung to my side, looking as unnerved as I felt. Luckily, I'd managed to find some concealment charms, so we could hide ourselves if necessary. Granted, the charms were pretty old, so they may no longer have magick.

I wasn't about to tell Abby that though.

"This is another stupid idea, Jordyn," she muttered under her breath.

"Probably," I admitted, hoping it came across as a

joke.

"We're not going to get caught are we?"

"We have our charms," I reminded her, hoping that I sounded confident.

"Right."

She didn't sound convinced, so I changed the subject. "It's strange, isn't it?"

"What is?"

Through the trees, we saw the town of Centerburg below. "If Zach was the one who killed David and Shea last night, he'd have to drive all the way out here to kill them."

Abby gave me a sidelong glance. "So you don't think he did it?"

"No, I don't think he did it. It seems too premeditated for him."

"Did you do it?"

The question stung and I couldn't keep the hurt from my face.

"Kidding, Jordyn." She sighed, putting her hands on her hips. "I know you didn't do it."

There wasn't really anything left of the crime from last night, other than the yellow police tape. I'm not sure what I expected, but I should have known that there wouldn't be anything here. Why did Zach want me coming up here then?

"Do you know what killed David and Shea last night? Like the murder weapon?" Abby asked. Her voice was as soft as the night air.

"They wouldn't tell me," I said. "I think they were waiting to see if I would guess. To try and use that against me."

"I'm sure *most* of the cops were," another voice said to my left.

I shrieked and whirled with my flashlight to see who it was. The light blinded our visitor and he held up a hand to block his eyes.

"Luke?" I asked hopefully, my voice wavering. Dammit, I guess this means that the concealment charms are too old to work.

"Yeah, it's me," he said, sounding unhappy. "Can you put the light down?"

"What are you doing here?" My heart hammered in my throat.

He squinted at me. "Can you please lower that light?"

"Sorry." I tilted my flashlight down.

Luke sighed and combed a hand through his hair. "Zach came home very agitated," he explained. "Slammed the door and everything. Woke me up, but he wouldn't answer any of my questions, except that you were heading out here. I got worried about you."

"So you followed us?" Abby snapped.

"Yeah."

It was so suspicious. After all, I'd left my jacket in Luke's car.

Then, I remembered that he was a cop. And I also

remembered how bad it must have looked that I was at the crime scene. Didn't serial killers always return to the scene of a crime?

I could tell that he thought the same of me. He looked wary and freaked out, and I noticed that his hand wasn't too far from his sidearm.

"Why are you here, Jordyn?"

"I'm just trying to figure out what happened."

"What happened?" Luke echoed. "Two people died horrible deaths. You two should get home. Before you get into trouble."

Abby's grip on my arm tightened, imploring me to leave.

I kept my feet planted firmly. "Not until I get some answers."

"Jordyn, you—"

"Luke, don't you want to know what happened to Zach?"

"What *did* happen to Zach?" he asked, his tone clipped.

"Something very bad," I said. "Something that reared its ugly head last night."

Luke groaned. "Jordyn, you could get in so much trouble if anyone else found out you were here."

"Not if I don't have anything to hide."

My eyes met his unwavering gaze. "I can't allow you to be out here," he said finally. "You're making this really hard."

"I'm not trying to. I'm really not, Luke."

We were at an impasse. Luke wanted me to go and I refused to move. Abby was looking between us wildly, and I could tell that she wanted us to leave as soon as possible.

Then I heard it, the *shhick* of something whispering in the air. I felt the prick of something on the back of my neck and I swatted at it, initially thinking that a mosquito had bitten me. However, when my fingers felt the feathers of a dart, my instincts went into overdrive, even as the drug hit my veins.

"What the—?" I slurred, fighting the overwhelming urge to close my eyes.

At first, I thought that Luke had betrayed me, until I saw both Abby and Luke pull at their necks, each now punctured with a dart. Neither of them had shot the darts, which my fading mind recognized as a relief. How smart was our attacker to do something like that? If I had any sort of warning, I could have tried to deflect the darts with magick.

Abby was the first to fall. Then Luke.

As I collapsed to the forest floor, my vision fading, I saw two slippered feet come into view.

Slippered feet?

"You're not supposed to be here," an angry voice snapped. I had heard that voice before. Recently. I struggled, trying to figure out who it was but my thoughts were fuzzy and my brain was like syrup. It was coming to me, but oh so slowly.

"Dammit, fall asleep, *witch*!"

Dimly, I felt the slight prick of another dart. While my mind pieced together the puzzle, darkness overcame me. My last thought was reaching through the void and calling for Zach, even though I knew it was impossible for him to hear me.

***

A SLAP BROUGHT ME BACK TO CONSCIOUSNESS.

"Ow!" I grimaced, spittle flying. I landed on my side, the hard floor knocking the wind out of me.

"You're pathetic," the voice lamented. "Get up!"

I felt like I was trying to think through cotton. *That voice is so familiar.* Blindfolded, the drug-induced haze clouded the rest of my senses.

Hard, splintery wood floors beneath me. My hands bound behind my back.

Where in the hell am I?

I cried out as a foot connected with my abdomen. Thankfully, there wasn't a boot attached to that foot, and it still wore the slipper from before. Still, it hurt, and I curled in a ball from the pain.

"I told you to get up, *Jordyn!*" the voice hissed.

Clarity struck me like lightning. I'd heard that voice so many times in my childhood. Telling me to quiet down, complaining to the police when my birthday party got too loud, griping at my aunt when I got too feisty.

Get off the grass, Jordyn.

My property starts here, Jordyn. Mow on your side.

Your mailbox is unsightly, Jordyn.

Your trash has been out too long, Jordyn.

It's too late for Christmas decorations, Jordyn.

"M—Mr. Samson?"

The air was sucked out of the space. I heard a resigned sigh, followed by a chuckle that oddly reminded me of Zach's crazy laugh. It was definitely Mr. Samson, even though I could count on one finger the number of times I'd heard him laugh.

This was the only time.

"Think you're so clever, don't you, witch?" he sneered. "Thinking you're better than me. Just like Margaret."

"Aunt Margaret?" I coughed. "What?"

"Jordyn?"

"*Abby?!*" I thrashed about wildly, trying to get loose to get my little sister. "ABBY?!"

One thing I could say about the old man; he was great at tying knots. I remembered him sitting on his porch, a length of rope in his hands and those gnarly old hands folding and knotting them. He'd been practicing, the bastard.

Those same hands seized me by the armpits and hauled me to my feet. When had Mr. Samson gotten so strong? I'd seen him yesterday, and he'd been old and frail.

What the hell was happening?

He plucked the blindfold from my eyes, disorienting

me. We were in a cabin, one like I'd expect to see in a stereotypical horror movie. Bare, untreated wooden walls surrounded us. A single incandescent lightbulb hanging from the ceiling illuminated the claustrophobic space. There were a few windows somewhat covered by tattered curtains, two doors, and a stone fireplace. A single faded couch faced the fireplace with a threadbare rug in front of it and a small kitchenette in the corner. There was a gun on the counter which I recognized as Luke's sidearm. So he was weaponless.

Then my eyes landed on the wall of…blades? Knives, swords, saws, pliers, box cutters—anything that could do some serious damage.

Did I wake up on the set of *Saw*?

On the wall opposite me, Abby was blindfolded like I had been, and she was bound hand and foot. She cowered against the wall, as disoriented as I'd been. Luke was splayed next to her, tied up too. He hadn't woken up yet. At least, I hoped he'd wake up. What if he was dead?

Think fast, Jordyn. Except I was so freaked out, I couldn't really concentrate on anything other than the fear.

"Where are we?" I asked. This wasn't Mr. Samson's house, that much I knew for sure. I'd been there once when I was in elementary school. My school had a fundraiser where we were required to sell fifty candy bars. Mom had forbidden me to go to Mr. Samson's house, but at that point, I was so ostracized by my classmates that I would have done anything to fit in. If that meant selling a bunch of chocolate to him, I'd risk it. I remembered that the walls of his house were covered with faded wallpaper and it smelled of mildew and despair.

This wasn't the same house. This one smelled of dirt and condemnation.

Wait. There was dirt, which meant I could tap into my magick. Yet, even as I thought that, I realized that the fear was paralyzing my powers. I couldn't get ahold of the magick, and my mind was mentally scrambling to try and build it up.

The old man leered over me and I saw how many teeth he was missing as his awful breath struck me head on. "Welcome to my summer house."

His tone was harsh, unforgiving. He wasn't being sarcastic or bemused.

"What are we doing here?"

He reached out and gripped my chin, inspecting me. "Sixty years," he said. "It's been almost sixty years since your bitch of an aunt ruined my life."

"*What?*"

His gaze had gone fuzzy, and I could tell that he mentally went back to whatever time period he was talking about.

Abby whimpered. Good thing she couldn't see the way that Mr. Samson had touched me, or the way he was now looking at me. Had he always looked at me like this? Or was this something new since I came back?

"You look like her, you know," Mr. Samson said,

his voice so low I could barely hear it. "The same face. The same expressions. The same fierce spirit. The same spirit that ruined my life." His eyes flicked to my hair, and he forcibly released me. "Your hair's not the same though. That awful pink. It's unnatural, like your whole family."

He turned away from me, his expression cruel. He stalked over to Abby, and even his slippers made the floorboards creak. Abby jerked away from the noise with a shriek. I was worried that he was going to terrorize her.

I have to find a way out of here.

The good thing about this space was that I could sense Earth nearby. If I could calm my racing heart and get myself to think straight, I could call up a spell and blast his ass, and then run away. If only it was easy as that. I could fight Zach and blast him away because I knew it was merely my life on the line. With Abby and Luke here, I could get all three of us hurt, and that thought was messing with my connection to nature.

I had to keep him focused on me.

"Mr. Samson," I appealed, "why are you doing this?"

"I told you," he said, without looking my way. "Margaret ruined my life."

"Yes, but…" A chill ran down my spine. "*How* did she ruin your life?"

At first, I didn't think the old man would answer. But I'd stumped him and he stopped his advance on Abby. When he spoke, his voice was as dry as autumn leaves.

"She's up here," he said. He tapped on his temple,

and I felt like I was watching a replay of last night with Zach. "She's up here and I can't get rid of her."

I gulped back the lump forming in my throat. "Can't get rid of her?" I asked gently, quivering on the inside.

"No," the old man spat. "She's my constant companion. Even when she snubs me."

I remembered how Aunt Margaret never wanted us to go near Mr. Samson. She lived a few houses down, but she was always over at our house. Protecting us.

What had happened between them?

"I can't leave Centerburg," the old man continued. "Not when she's so close by. This cabin is my church where I worship her. And my prison where *she* is my punishment."

There was a window to my left. I sidled up to it, and nudged the curtain open to get a better look of where we were. We certainly weren't in my neighborhood.

When I saw what was outside, I screamed, backpedaling away from the window.

Outside the window was a dilapidated carport, where I could see the silhouette of a huge black truck underneath in the darkness. It had been three years since I last saw that truck last, and even though the headlights had been on and it had been traveling at forty miles per hour that night, I recognized it now.

Memories flooded back to me, every single detail of that night, unfortunately too late to help identify the truck. It all came back, the height and shape of the headlights. How there was a large crack across the windshield, made even larger by Zach's body hitting it.

That truck killed Zach.

Mr. Samson didn't flinch at my scream. Instead, he gave me a knowing, evil grin.

"*You,*" I growled.

"Me."

"*You* killed Zachary." My voice came out strangled and tears fell down my cheeks, though I only dimly felt them. Every fiber of my being was once again mourning the loss of Zach, of *us*.

"Killed?" Mr. Samson shook his head, confused. "No, he's alive. I just saw him."

I clenched my jaw. "You killed him," I repeated through my clenched teeth. "Zachary Harington, the boy who grew up next door to you. You killed him in cold blood."

Saying it out loud made it worse. My stomach roiled.

Mr. Samson shook his head again, harder. "No. He's alive."

Luke stirred, finally waking up. Abby's eyes were entirely too wide when I met them. In that brief moment, I silently pleaded with her. She swallowed nervously and scooted over towards Luke.

Luke, come on. Open your eyes!

I steered my gaze back towards Mr. Samson, who was sneering at me. I needed to focus and think of the appropriate spell to subdue him, while keeping his attention away from Abby and Luke. My rustiness and my fear were messing with my magick.

"You murdered Zach," I said.

"I tried to. He was too close to you. You are mine."

"*Me?* Why?"

"Because you are the spitting image of her," Mr. Samson said. "After all these years, you will be my prize for waiting so patiently." He stroked the side of my check.

I felt sick. "So you killed Zach so you could have me?"

He laughed lowly. "I wasn't trying to *kill* Zach, Margaret. I was trying to keep you."

"I'm not Margaret," I said.

"You are her doppelganger," he declared, no emotion in his voice. "The hair. Your face. You are mine."

Oh my god. He believed me to be Margaret, therefore I was.

"I'm Jordyn," I said through gritted teeth. "And I'm no one's."

He roughly grabbed me by the face again. I winced as he hauled me away from the window. "You are Margaret!" he shrieked, spit flying in my face. "You will be my Margaret!"

He was insane.

"Hey!"

Mr. Samson whirled at the voice, snarling. Luke was awake. Disoriented, but awake. He glared up at the older man.

"Don't you dare touch her like that again!" Luke

yelled. "Leave. Her. Alone."

The old man blinked at him in confusion, taking his attention off me for just long enough. The spell finally came to my mind and I shouted it at the top of my lungs, putting all of my willpower into the words.

"Tremble and shake, suffer and quiver
Stay away 'til I'll banish you again!"

The magick moved through me, like a tsunami of power filling up in my chest. A blast of green power hit the old man, blowing him away. He crashed into the far side of the cabin, behind the couch by the kitchenette, and out of sight.

I stood there, breathing harshly for a few moments, the blood roaring through my ears. I did it. I had used an offensive spell.

My hearing came back all at once, and someone was shouting at me.

"…dyn! Jordyn!"

Abby.

I turned back to the two of them, and Abby was sobbing while Luke…well, he looked at me like I was some sort of alien creature. He'd never seen me use magick before, and seeing this was probably one heck of an introduction.

I scrambled over to him. "Untie me," I commanded, turning away and offering up my tied up hands. He didn't move initially. "Untie me, dammit!"

Luke finally snapped out of it and grunted in answer,

situating himself so he could get access to my arms. It was awkward trying to untie ourselves this way, but I couldn't see any other way of getting out of this. He had to crane his head around to see what his hands were doing, and it couldn't have been comfortable.

"What was Mr. Samson talking about, Jordyn?" Abby whined.

"I don't know."

"You…you blasted him away," Luke grimaced, his hands slipping as the rope painfully bit into my wrists. "Dammit."

"There's some truth to what everyone's been accusing us of," I told him blandly, positioning to allow for more leverage against my binds. "I'm a witch and I use magick. It just saved your life."

He gave a mirthless chuckle at that. "What am I going to tell the guys at the station?"

"That you arrested the killer from last night," I answered. I met his eyes, holding him there. "And you're going to clear my name. No more magick needed. I told you I didn't kill David and Shea."

Our gazes locked and he held me there, giving me a slow nod.

"Jordyn!" Abby screamed. "*Jordyn!*"

I felt the impact of the frying pan hit my cheekbone before the pain spread throughout my body. With a loud clang, I was hurtled aside, stars and blackness danced across my vision. Mr. Samson stood over me, huffing loudly with the pan raised, poised to strike again. Abby was screaming while Luke was shouting at him to turn his attention their way.

Admirable, but the old man only had eyes for me.

"You tease me by looking like Margaret," the old man snarled. "Then you show up after three years, and I *had* to do something about it last night. No more happy endings. Not for anyone. Not for you. Not for Margaret. Not for those two screwing in the backyard of my summer house."

A motive for murder. Part of me realized that I was partly responsible for David and Shea's demise, because my presence had impacted the old man that much. If only I had known.

He held the frying pan aloft, ready to strike again when the door to the outside was splintered open, breaking apart. In the shadows stood...

Zach.

Somehow, he had found his way here. Whether he had heard me when I had passed out earlier or it was a lucky guess, he was here now. I hadn't been so happy to see him in a long time.

He looked huge, intimidating, and ghastly standing in the doorway like that. This was the scary, dead Zach that had terrorized me at night, and had scared Abby and my family. He looked both fragile and unbreakable at the same time, innocent and evil. Those shark-like eyes fell upon our neighbor and he grinned like a dead man.

"You killed me," he said. His voice reverberated

throughout the cabin, filling it with his presence. "You killed me that night."

Mr. Samson turned on Zach, the frying pan clattering to the floor. "I didn't kill you!" he screamed. "You're standing right here!"

Zach moved up to him at lightning speed. "There are different ways of being dead, old man. Some worse than others." His eyes flicked to me when he said that, and my stomach churned at the unspoken blame.

Mr. Samson reeled away from him, but Zach was there to counter him, leering over him like some sort of specter.

"You killed me," he cackled. "You killed me!" He kept repeating it, his voice getting shriller and shriller each time, faster and faster. I wished that my hands were untied if only to cover my ears.

"I did not kill you!" Mr. Samson screamed in defense. "You are right here!"

"Youkilledmeyoukilledmeyoukilledme!"

"I wanted Margaret!" Mr. Samson finally screamed, edging up to the wall. "I only wanted Margaret!"

That made Zach stop his chanting. "See, that doesn't work either. Because she's MINE!"

He barreled into the old man, pushing him up against the wall. They stood there, frozen for a few seconds, before Zach took a shuddering breath and staggered away, clutching at his chest. Red blossomed between his fingers and it was only then that I saw the knife. Mr. Samson started laughing, a low laugh, which was somehow worse than any other noise I'd heard that whole night.

In between my blasting him over the couch and Zach arriving, Mr. Samson had picked up the Bowie knife that was now sticking out of Zach's chest.

"No!" I screamed, thrashing about. My mind couldn't…wouldn't work. No spells came to mind, only pain, and fear about doing something worse.

I was watching Zach die a second time, and it was only now that I realized how much I loved him.

I started sobbing.

"I killed you now!" Mr. Samson spat. "I killed you *now*, boy!"

The earsplitting crack of gunfire filled the cabin. Mr. Samson's eyes went wide beneath a bullet hole in his forehead and he teetered backwards himself. He collapsed against the walls, spluttering blood as he slid down, painting the wood a dark red.

A fatal gunshot wound.

Mr. Samson wasn't going to kill anyone else now.

I looked behind me to see Luke standing, holding his sidearm. He had somehow untied his bonds and found his gun on the kitchenette counter. Maybe because he'd been trying to untie his bounds before I came over earlier or maybe because seeing his little brother battle an unhinged old man was enough to make him tear through it.

Our eyes met for the briefest moment before he said one word: "Zach."

With my hands still toed behind me, I scrambled over to Zach's body.

"Zach!" I cried. "Zach!"

My ex-boyfriend lay on the on floor, both hands wrapped around the knife sticking out of his chest. He was dying. Again. Whatever magick I had infused him with the night he died was seeping away, like water through my fingertips.

I was losing Zach. Again.

"This is what I wanted, Jordyn," he said. "Don't cry…" Gone was the demented, *wrong* version of Zach that we'd been living with for the past three years. This was the Zach that I grew up with, the one I loved, the one who loved me.

My Zach.

Luke was at my side then, untying my bounds. Impatience scrapped at my resolve and when my hands were finally free, I forced myself to be gentle when all I wanted to do was meld with him to bring him back. He was supposed to be with me.

"I'm so sorry, Zach!" I cried. "I ruined everything. I shouldn't have brought you back, I—"

"Shhh," Zach crooned. His eyes fluttered closed. "You couldn't have known…"

"I wanted you back. I wanted you back!" I wanted to pound the floor in anger, do something, *anything* to change the past to change our futures. If only I could have spotted that our neighbor was psycho. If only I could have fought the urge to run back to our car that night. If only I didn't love him so much.

He might still be alive.

"You gave me three more years," Zach said. "You found yourself... Don't regret that..."

A wracking shudder ripped through his body.

"I love you, Zachary Harington."

A smile quirked up on the edges of his lips. "Ditto," he whispered, referencing our favorite scene from *Ghost*. We had watched it together tons of times. Zach had always thought it was a sappy movie, but he never minded watching it with me. His turn of phrase only served to make me cry harder. "But you'll have someone else to love you," he added dreamily.

He coughed again.

I kissed his lips, trying to will him back to me. I didn't want to bring him back—not if he was going to be the *wrong* version of him. I wanted him the way we used to be, and that wasn't going to happen.

Even at his worst, he still saved us. He died a hero. Like he always had been.

When he died in my arms, it came in two waves. At first, I felt the dark power leave him like the tide going out. The power and the presence that had inhabited his body for three years left. I don't know what it was, whether it was a demon that reanimated him or my own dark magick. But it left him, leaving my Zach looking up at me.

And then he was gone.

Leaving me alone in the world again.

CHAPTER 9

ABBY CLUNG TO ME WHILE WE WAITED IN the back of an ambulance. Though we had blankets wrapped around us, I felt colder than I'd ever been before. I kept replaying everything, wondering what I could have done differently.

The police had arrived in a flurry of red and blue lights, too late to change the past; too late to alter the future. We gave our statements each in turn. And through it all, Luke wouldn't look at me, whether it was from the shock of killing Mr. Samson or my part in why Zach's life had been ruined, I couldn't tell.

Now that we were outside, I saw that we were a hundred yards from Lake Asbury, near Shady Point. Apparently Mr. Samson kept a secluded cabin out in the forest that no one knew about. The truck—the weapon that killed Zach—was suspected to have been stolen from Jacksonville about six years ago.

What was even more disturbing, cops found evidence that we weren't the first people Mr. Samson had kidnapped and kept in his little cabin. With his non-descript car, he appeared to have been able to travel in a wide radius and steal people off the streets. They wouldn't give me any more details, but before our very eyes, the two squad cars had grown to over twelve, and some very important-looking people with badges went into the cabin.

Sunlight was beginning to seep through the trees when Aunt Margaret's old Honda Civic pulled up to the cabin. She emerged from the driver's side, a frown on her face, and anger encroached on my vision. If only she had told me, Zach may still be alive.

Then I saw the passenger door open, and my mother stepped out of the car. She looked pale and wobbly, but she gave me a small smile and nodded.

She was well. Zach's passing had rid her of the burden of keeping him bound.

Blind joy brought me to my feet and I ran to her, my blanket dropping to the forest floor. Abby ran alongside me, and our mother wrapped us up in a hug. The three of us collapsed on the ground crying.

Mom was going to be all right.

Aunt Margaret shushed one of the police officers, telling them to call us if they needed anything.

I was with my mother, my sister, and my great aunt. My family. Suddenly, the future didn't seem so bleak.

After three years, I finally had hope.

***

"HAVE SOME CAKE, JORDYN."

Aunt Margaret set down a chocolate slice in front of me from the cake I made the day before. I glanced out the window, checking that it was still morning.

It had been a long night.

"For breakfast?" I asked, picking up my fork.

"I think we've all learned that life's too short," Aunt Margaret said, taking a seat opposite me on the island with her own slice of cake.

I couldn't agree more.

When we got home, Abby had gone directly to bed, citing exhaustion. Mom had followed her, saying that she was still recovering from her illness. She said she felt like she had the flu. For some reason, that hadn't been funny to me though she laughed like it was the best joke she's heard in ages.

I popped a forkful of cake in my mouth. Aunt Margaret watched me with her keen eyes.

"So you're back to being a witch," she said shortly.

"Yes. I suppose I am."

The small talk was killing me. That's all I had been doing with Aunt Margaret since she picked us up. I hadn't brought it up in front of Mom because I didn't want to upset her, but I *had* to know.

"Ask, Jordyn," she commanded, digging into her own slice of cake.

"What happened between you and Mr. Samson?"

A pained look washed over my great aunt's face. It appeared as though her wrinkles suddenly popped out and she was ten years older.

"Stephen," she said. "His name is…*was* Stephen." She sighed. "Surely you've gotten the impression that Stephen hasn't ever left Centerburg?"

I nodded. He had that small town mentality that all the rest of the townies had. If anything, my travels with Neptune and the other mermaids had taught me that there was so much more to this world, even if all I wanted was to go home.

"We grew up together."

Like Zach and me.

"Like Zachary and you," she agreed, as if reading my mind. "I loved him so much. But this was in a time where everyone ostracized us horribly for being witches. You think you grew up with superstitions and prejudice? You should have been there in the fifties. You and Zachary had a connection that you could build on for the future; Stephen treated me like I was lower than dirt. And he wasn't the only one, everyone in town treated us like lepers."

Her voice was bitter, and, as if she needed something sweet to help with the taste in her mouth, she had another bite of her cake. The look on her face was that of disgust.

"I did what any girl would have done—I cast a love spell."

My mouth dropped open. "That's dark magick."

"I know. Funny how you don't care about that stuff when you're sixteen. You understand, I'm sure."

I didn't give her the satisfaction of agreeing with her.

"I cast a love spell on him, and it worked," she added. "Too well. He followed me around, became obsessed with me. At first I loved it, that he was finally seeing me for the first time. He wanted to be around me, even when everyone else treated me as if I had some sort of disease. It was wonderful for about six months. We loved each other. *He* loved me and that was all that mattered. Or so I thought."

She got up from the island and refilled her coffee mug. When she came back to sit down, her eyes were filled with tears. "It became too much one day. I wanted Stephen's fiery spirit back, because whatever that was inside him, it wasn't Stephen. *My* Stephen was funny, had his own outside interests. He wanted to be a doctor. The Stephen he'd turned into wasn't any of those things. So I tried removing the spell."

I remembered what she had said when I wanted to do something for Zach, to reverse or lessen the effects the spell had on him. I wanted to remove whatever had twisted him into something else. Aunt Margaret had looked like she was terrified. Now I understood why.

"The spell didn't work. If anything, it only accelerated what happened. He became angry, refused to stop loving me. He wanted to spend his whole life with me, and I didn't want to anymore. It twisted him into some sort of person, something that I didn't recognize. That's the thing, even when I had him, I realized that I didn't want him anymore. I was a terrible person.

"So I put a binding spell on him. Not as powerful as

the one your mother put on Zach, but one to keep him at a distance, even to try and give him a happy life. Only I didn't realize he was capable of all that he has done."

"What was the price?"

She looked at me in confusion. "What?"

"The price. For binding him. Mom binding Zach nearly killed her. For you…?"

Aunt Margaret gave me a half-hearted smile. "The price was my own happiness. I never got married or fell in love with anyone after I put the binding spell on Stephen."

"So while Mom's binding spell gave her cancer," I asked incredulously, "yours took away your happy ending?"

"Never underestimate the value of happiness," Aunt Margaret warned. "It's all that any of us work for in our lives. Mine impacted my life in a way that I couldn't have known at the time."

"Was that why you didn't want me to take off the spell or do anything with Zach?" I said. "Because you'd been there yourself?"

"Yes."

"Why didn't you leave Centerburg like I did?"

"This was a different kind of magick, Jordyn. It wasn't as powerful as the one you put on Zach, though you'd think that love and reincarnation would be closely aligned. Plus, your grandmother and your mom were here, and I didn't want to leave family behind. Stephen stayed, too. While he never crossed that boundary to attack us, he never wanted to leave us either." She chuckled bitterly. "I thought I had it under control."

"You didn't," I said. I was not accusing her, only stating the fact. "You didn't have it under control at all."

She nodded, resigned. "I realize that now. I feel like the deaths of the people he killed are on me."

"Why did he attack us that night when Zach died? Why did he kill David and Shea?"

"Let me get something really quick," Aunt Margaret said. She got up from the island, disappearing into another part of the house for a few minutes. When she came back, she had a tattered photograph that she put in front of me.

In the frayed, sepia-toned photograph, wearing fifties fashion and sitting on a porch, *I* was smiling back at me. It took me aback.

"Everyone always said you looked like me," Aunt Margaret said.

No wonder Mr. Samson accused me of looking like Aunt Margaret. Or why my pink hair color had bothered him. I looked exactly like Aunt Margaret had a long time ago.

"So when he killed Zach…?"

"He must have either been trying to kill you. Or," my great aunt shuddered, "he wanted to keep you."

"What about David and Shea? And leaving my jacket at the scene?"

"Obviously, your presence set him off-kilter again."

"Off kilter?" I asked sardonically. "He killed two people!"

"That's the only real way to explain what he did, Jordyn. And he might have left your jacket on the scene on purpose, to frame you, or to get back at me. Something. You can't understand craziness."

"What about the other people he killed?" I asked, my voice rough.

Aunt Margaret was silent for a long time before answering. "I feel responsible for each and every one of those deaths. But Stephen ultimately was the one who committed those crimes. That's the thing you have to remember—he did those himself."

"Is that how you're able to sleep at night?" I snapped. "Because I feel responsible for everything that Zach did."

"Just be glad that he didn't kill someone," Aunt Margaret replied. "I always told you that you were a powerful witch, Jordyn. I wish I could have protected you from the same mistakes I made."

"Yeah, well…"

The doorbell rang. Aunt Margaret and I looked at each other for a few heartbeats before I sighed and got off my barstool.

"Tell him I said hi," Aunt Margaret said. "And, Jordyn, I hope you find your happiness."

I didn't know what she meant until I opened the door. Luke stood before me, looking like he hadn't slept, showered, or changed clothes. He didn't look too happy to see me either.

"Can we talk?"

I stepped out of the house. It was around eight o'clock in the morning and the sun hadn't yet vaporized the chill in the morning air. I crossed my arms in front of my chest to retain some body heat.

"So you're a real witch," Luke said, unable to keep the accusation from his voice. "Like everyone says."

I flinched. "Yes."

"And you sacrificed Zach? Is that why he was acting weird?"

"No!" I said in horror. "No. Mr. Samson, he, uh, killed Zach. You remember when we went to the hospital after junior prom that night?"

Luke's jaw clenched. "I remember. That was the night Zach started acting weird."

"Zach was killed that night, Luke. I brought him back from the dead. I loved him so much that I couldn't see beyond my pain. I only wanted to bring him back the way he was. But when he came back, he was different."

"Yes," Luke agreed, his voice harsh. "You have no idea how awful it was living with that. We thought he had snapped or had brain damage or something."

"No. It was me, trying to bring him back to me."

"How?"

"Magick." No sense in trying to candy coat it. "I dabbled in some magick that I shouldn't have to bring him back."

I could see his teeth grinding. "Why?"

I blinked at him. "Because I loved him." *Still love him.*

"I couldn't imagine a world without him."

Digesting this, Luke frowned at me. "So why did Mr. Samson want to kill him?"

I gave him a pained look. "Because he wanted to get to me."

Luke waited for me to continue, but I didn't say anything else. I stood there with tears spilling over my cheeks.

"So you mean to tell me that Mr. Samson had an obsession with you? And that's why he killed so many people?"

I grimaced. "Yeah."

"Bullshit." When I didn't say anything else, Luke exploded. "You have to tell me more than that, Jordyn. You *owe* me that. I had to kill a man today. I had to watch my baby brother die, a different man from what he was, but he was still my little brother." He nodded with his head towards his house. "I had to tell my parents that Zach was dead. Killed by a crazy man."

"He *was* killed by a crazy man," I said. "Both times. My family has made mistakes, Luke, and I'm so sorry about that, but I didn't kill him."

Luke licked his lips, a faraway gaze in his eyes. "So what do we do now?" he asked.

"I don't know."

"You damn well better know, Jordyn," Luke snapped. "Did you put a spell on me?"

It stung that he would think that, but I suppose it was

warranted. "No."

"I'm not sure I believe you," Luke answered. "Because *this* isn't going away."

"What isn't?"

He sucked in a deep breath. "I will have to think on this," he said. "Are you going to stick around, or are you going back to being a mermaid?"

"I don't know." I hadn't even thought that far ahead yet. My plan was originally to do that. But then again, everything had changed, hadn't it?

"I'm sure my partner won't want you leaving Centerburg."

I laughed and shook my head. Officer Pratt probably wanted me burned at the stake. "That's not why I'd want to stay, Luke."

"I need to think," Luke said, distractedly. "To figure out what to do next."

"So do I," I admitted.

The awkward silence that followed was the hardest silence that I'd ever experienced. We stood there, not looking at each other. Finally, Luke exhaled.

"I'll let you go back inside. Your mom probably needs you."

"She's better now."

Rather than be happy, his jaw clenched. "Of course," he said. "You're witches. You make everything better for yourselves. What about the rest of us?"

When he left me on the porch, I sobbed until my ribs hurt.

***

I'D GONE UP TO CUDDLE WITH MOM AND sleep some more, but I couldn't rest. I hadn't made anything better for myself. If anything, I'd screwed up things beyond repair.

Luke's words continued to haunt me, about what I'd do next. I could go back to being a part of Neptune's Mermaids, or I could stay home, like I'd been wanting to for the last three years.

I'd spent the last three years trying not to be a witch. And now that I was here, I had no idea what I wanted to do or be.

I simply wanted to be Jordyn. Was that so much to ask?

I couldn't call Christine or Alaina about it. I was sure they'd give me a biased opinion, and tell me that I had to go back to them. Though a part of me *did* want to go back, a part of me wanted to stay here, to begin my life over again.

There was one other person that I could call, and though I'd only known her a short time, and much of that was away from the troupe, I knew that she could give me perspective. If she wasn't busy. Studying marine biology, apparently, was a lot of work, and she was gone most weekends.

I stared at my phone for a full minute before pulling her contact information: Tara Porter, the girl who had been a part of Neptune's Mermaids for only two months. Who suddenly left to go to college for the spring semester.

I dialed, closed my eyes, and hit "SEND".

The phone rang three times, each pulse agonizing. I didn't think she was going to pick up, then Tara's familiar voice answered.

"Hello?"

"Hey, Tara, it's Jordyn."

"Jordyn!" She sounded genuinely excited to hear from me. "How are you doing?"

"I'm doing all right," I said, reverting to the usual greeting for the question. Then I shook my head, realizing that she couldn't see me. "I mean, no. I'm doing all right, I guess. I've had quite the past few days, and now I'm debating what to do. You know?"

There was a pause on her end. "I do know what you mean," she said. "You've had one of those kinds of weeks that change everything in your life? Where you look at the next phase in your life and wonder what you should do?"

"Yeah."

"Are you thinking about leaving Neptune's Mermaids?"

I rubbed at my eyes. "Yes. How did you know it was time for you to leave?"

"Well, I had a weekend that made me look at

everything differently. And I realized my purpose."

Tara had acted weird for a couple of days before she quit. She disappeared all because she met some boy she fell in love with, though I suspected that wasn't all that happened. After all, she kind of went crazy and set a dolphin free. I wouldn't be surprised if she told me she was a witch too.

"What was the purpose of your life?" I asked.

"To be happy. And I found how I could do that."

"Are you happy now?"

"Yes, Jordyn. I'm very happy."

I sat down with a groan, knowing what was coming next. "I guess I have to make a phone call to Neptune."

She laughed. "I'm happy for you too, Jordyn."

"It's not a happy ending," I said, blinking back tears. I'd been with the mermaids about two years longer than Tara. Neptune, Christine, and Alaina were as much of a family to me as Mom, Aunt Margaret, and Abby. It was going to be hard leaving them forever.

"It will be," Tara said, sounding sure of it.

It was time for Jordyn Murphy to move on with her life. It was time to start anew. It was time for me to fully embrace being a witch again.

"Tell them I said hi, would you?" Tara asked.

"I will. Hey, Tara?"

"Yes?"

"Are…are you a witch? I mean, you did something to that dolphin for it to jump over the wall and into the ocean.

You set him free."

She chuckled. "No, Jordyn. I'm not a witch. I'm a mermaid who helped out a fellow sea creature in need."

I laughed with her. If I was a real witch, I suppose it was entirely possible that she was a real mermaid.

EPILOGUE

Three weeks later

"SO A *BOOK OF SHADOWS* CAN BE ANYTHING?" Abby asked me. "Even a three-ring binder?"

We were out in my family's backyard as the sun was setting. After quitting Neptune's Mermaids, I moved everything from my apartment in Jacksonville back to Mom's house. I was going to stay here for the moment and make up for lost time, which sounded perfect to me.

"Yep, a *Book of Shadows* can be anything." I told my little sister. She wasn't gifted as a witch, but I wanted to teach her everything I knew about being one. We were Murphy women, and we had to understand our family's legacy.

I took my purchases out of the bag: pre-hole punched stationary, salt, incense, a white candle, a bottle of water, a fancy pen, and the one item I was most excited about—a three-ring binder that featured an illustration of a mermaid in a body of water talking to a wood nymph under a tree. Water and Earth elements came together in a piece of art that represented who I was and who I wanted to be.

I couldn't believe that I'd found something so perfect for me, and at Wal-Mart of all places.

I needed to consecrate my new *Book of Shadows* before I could really feel like myself again. After three years of suppressing the witch side of me, I couldn't wait to fully reconnect with that part of myself.

"Stand over there," I told Abby. "After this, we'll get you to do it." We had a binder for her to create a *Book of Shadows* as well featuring Justin Bieber. I don't think she's taking it as seriously as I am.

She nodded, stepping back firmly on the porch. "You know mine won't work, right?"

"It will work."

As part of the consecration process, I had to offer my new *Book of Shadows* to each of the elements, starting with Earth. I felt most nervous for it, as it was *my* element.

I lit the candle and the incense, the scented smoke filling up the space. I took a deep breath and picked up my *Book of Shadows*.

I faced North, holding the binder over the salt, saying the incantation:

> *"Magick of the North,*
> *Guardians of the Earth,*
> *I consecrate my Book of Shadows*
> *and ask for your energies.*
> *I purify and make this tool sacred."*

The earthy smell of moss, wood, and grass wafted up. I inhaled it, feeling at peace. I couldn't keep the grin off my face. I followed the same format with the other three elements and the incense, candle, and water, and then I held the binder to the sky.

"I banish the energies of the previous owners and make it mine.

I consecrate this Book of Shadows."

I opened the first page and wrote with my fountain pen while saying aloud, "This the *Book of Shadows* of Jordyn Murphy, an Earth-based witch."

Once finished, I clutched my new *Book of Shadows* to my chest, bowing my head. The tears fell unbidden. I was on the right track to reconnecting with my past and I promised to never part with my *Book of Shadows* ever again.

This is who I am.

"You're crying," Abby called out lamely.

I grinned back at her. "Your turn."

Abby didn't look convinced.

"Even if you can't use magick," I said, getting to my feet, "you still need a *Book*. Now come out here and do it."

Abby looked like she was about to say something, then the door opened, revealing my mom standing with Luke. At first, I thought he was on police business—after all, with the way we left things, it *had* to be official business, right? Then I saw that he was in a t-shirt and jeans.

"You have a visitor, Jordyn," Mom said.

Suddenly, it felt like all the blood rushed to my cheeks. Other than a few dealings with the police, I hadn't seen him since the morning after Mr. Samson and Zach died.

He scratched at his head, that nervous habit that I recognized from growing up with him. "Hey, Jordyn. Uh, can we talk?"

Mom gave me an enigmatic smile. "Abby, why don't you come inside for a bit?"

"But I was just—" Mom gave her a sardonic smile that made Abby stop. "Oh, fine."

My little sister followed Mom into the house, leaving me with an awkward Luke.

"Did I interrupt you?" he asked nervously.

"No," I said. "I was finished."

"Doing what?"

"Creating a new *Book of Shadows*. I'm getting back in touch with my roots." I chuckled. "It's a witch thing."

"So you're staying in Centerburg?"

"For the moment, yeah. Mom's getting better and I need to be here for Abby." Not to mention that I had to keep an eye on Aunt Margaret too. She wasn't acting quite herself after finding out that Mr. Samson was a serial killer. News of what he'd done had hit the media and the stuff he did was like something out of a horror movie.

Aunt Margaret blamed herself, much like I had done with Zach. If anything, the past three weeks had taught me that free will wasn't a spell or anything you could cast.

Zach had been obsessed with me because he had loved me obsessively. Mr. Samson had killed those people because he was a murderer at heart, regardless of whatever spells had been put on him.

"I'd been doing a lot of thinking," Luke said. "About how we left things."

"Me too."

And I had. I don't know if it was because I suddenly had a bunch of free time or what, but whenever I had a moment, my thoughts drifted back to Luke. Who'd always been there for me. Who I had inexplicably let down.

"Did you do any magick on me too?" Luke asked, breaking into my thoughts.

"What do you mean?"

"You've cast a spell over me."

I was about to protest when he kissed me. It had been so long since I'd been kissed like this, it caught me off guard. At the same time, it was wonderful, I felt the Earth singing around me, humming in happiness. I closed my eyes, losing myself in it.

He grinned. Apparently, it had been just as good for him. "That kind of spell."

"I didn't."

"Hmmm. Then I should probably test it again."

He gave me a tender kiss, slowly pulling me to him. It grew more and more passionate the longer we held it.

No, Luke. You were the one who cast a spell on me.

We broke our kiss, and I looked at him, dazed.

"We'll take this slow," he whispered, stroking my cheek. "See if it's the right thing."

"Okay," I agreed. "Let's go inside, I think that chocolate cake Aunt Margaret was making is probably ready." She was using my recipe; I knew it was good.

"Don't want to be late for that," Luke said. "She kinda scares me."

I laughed and followed him inside. I took one last look around the backyard, remembering all of the times we played here, all of the times Zach came to see me, the flower bush. How many times had Mr. Samson watched me from here? I shuddered.

I wasn't sure if anything ever had been normal. Then again, when you're a witch, you *aren't* normal. And that's all right. I'd always been a witch, past and present.

And for now, that's all I wanted to be.

ACKNOWLEDGMENTS

My second outing in the world of *How to be a Mermaid* and *I'd Rather be a Witch* had a unique set of challenges that I wouldn't have been able to overcome without the help of some wonderful people in my life.

First of all, to my Nerd Crew, thank you for being there. You all rock.

The Blazing Indie Collective – every one of you is an inspiration and I'm proud to call you my friends and colleagues.

Special shout outs are in order for Emily, Lori, Lateia, and Felicia. You ladies keep me sane even when I fight hard to be insane.

Thank you to my friends, coworkers, and family. I love you guys.

Special thanks to my cat for not biting me too much while I was writing this.

And thank you to Chris. I wouldn't be able to do this without you.

THE WITCHING HOUR COLLECTION

Good witch. Bad witch. White magic. Black magic. Kitchen magic. Pick your potion. Ready for Halloween?

The authors of the Blazing Indie Collective, who brought you the Falling in Deep Collection, are brewing up something new. Check out all the novellas in The Witching Hour Collection coming October 2015:

Melanie Karsak: *Witch Wood*

Claire C. Riley: *Raven's Cove*

Eli Constant: *Sleeping in the Forest of Shadows*

Elizabeth Watasin: *Charm School: The Wrecking Faerie*

Erin Hayes: *I'd Rather be a Witch*

Carrie Wells: *Playing with Magic*

Evan Winters: *The Witch of Bracken's Hollow*

Minerva Lee: *Spun Gold*

Blaire Edens: *The Witch of Roan Mountain*

Poppy Lawless: *The Cupcake Witch*

The adventure continues for Alaina's baby in…

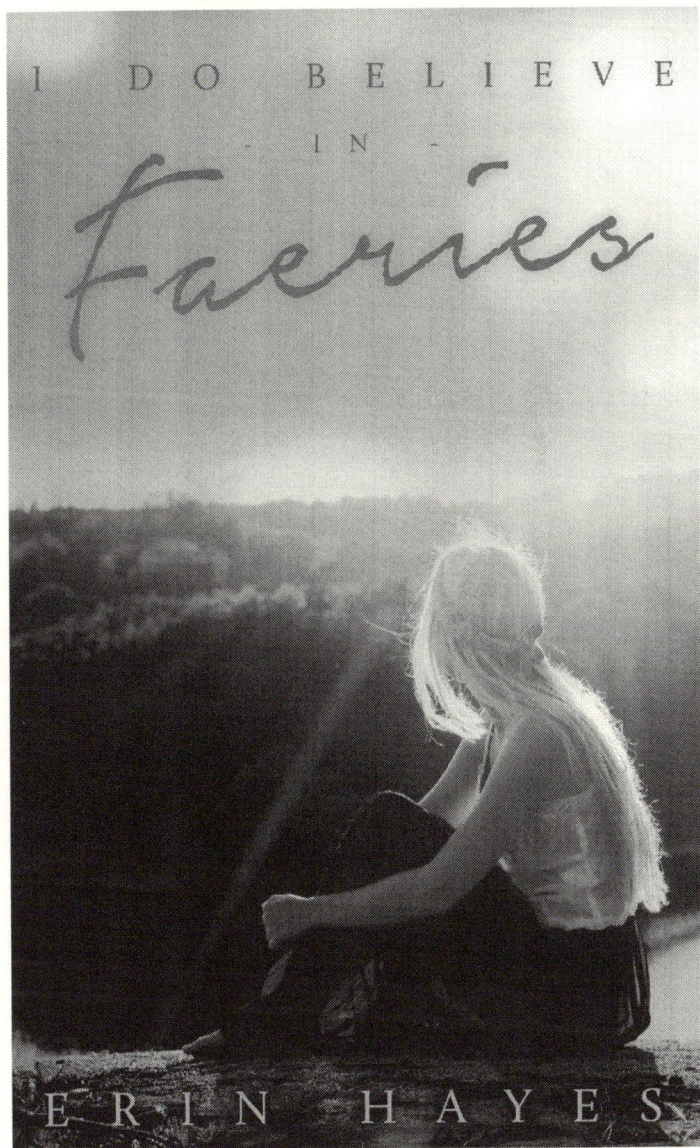

I DO BELIEVE
- IN -
Faeries

ERIN HAYES

Coming in Spring 2016 as part of
the Blazing Indie Collection Faerie Collection.

BONUS SNEAK PEEK:
HOW TO BE A MERMAID
by Erin Hayes

All Tara ever wanted was to be a mermaid.

So she takes a year off between high school and college to don a fake tail and tour aquariums across the country in a professional mermaid troupe.

Everything's great until she meets a gorgeous real-life merman named Finn. Suddenly, what she thought was a dream turns out to be a nightmare -- she's turning into a mermaid herself. For real.

Yet when she returns to the sea to seek out Finn and reverse her transformation, she finds herself in the middle of an impending war between the land and sea. Tara may have always wanted to be a mermaid, but now it's sink or swim. In order to survive, she has to learn how to be one, too.

ANYONE WHO EVER BRAGGED ABOUT BEING
a good public speaker never had to do it in front of more
than thirty kids and their parents while wearing a bikini top
and a mermaid tail.

I'd spent the night before in our hotel room preparing
my answers, and I still wasn't ready. I was sitting on a chair
in the rotunda of the Houston Aquarium, looking out into
a sea of faces and I'd never felt more self-conscious in
my life. My friend and fellow mermaid, Christine, stood to
my right, a little bit behind me with a few volunteers and
ushers from the aquarium to help out.

Every single eye was on me, and a barrage of
questions came at me from all directions. I've performed
our water ballet many times before, although this was the
first time I was face-to-face with a crowd. I was a dancer,
not a spokesperson.

As a result, my first meet and greet as a professional
mermaid was receiving a lot of scrutiny from a bunch of
kids under the age of eight.

"How are you on land?"

"Do you swim with whales?"

"Why isn't your hair red like Ariel's?"

"How old are you?"

"How did you become a mermaid?"

My answers didn't make much sense because my
nerves were getting the best of me. Throw me in the water,
and I can make you believe that mermaids are real. Expect
me to entertain a bunch of kids like this, and I drown.

"I was carried here by my helpers, that's how I'm on land. Sometimes I swim with Beluga whales... I have dark hair, while Ariel dyes hers. I just turned eighteen, and I've wanted to be a mermaid since I was a little girl..."

My voice trailed off as I realized that my last answer gave too much away, by nearly admitting that we weren't real mermaids. Christine shot me a concerned look, like I'd raised the curtain too much and these kids would be able to see behind it.

"What Mermaid Tara *means* is, she's so glad to be a mermaid," Christine said with a warm smile. She was a bit older than me, in her early thirties, and she was a good mentor for my first two months on the job.

The kids seemed to take her at her word, and my secret that I'd had a normal human childhood was safe.

Yet, despite Christine's save, what I'd said was true.

If you had asked me when I was little what I wanted to be when I grew up, I would have said "mermaid". If you had asked me now what I wanted to be when I was eighteen, I would have said "mermaid" as well. Unlike most girls, I was completely serious. Ever since I was three years old and my dad sat me on his lap to watch Disney's *The Little Mermaid*, I was enamored with the idea of being a creature of the sea and being able to swim in the water with absolute freedom. I wanted to see the beauty of the underwater world.

I was determined that somehow or another, I would be a mermaid.

My mother had tried to convince me to go into something more sensible. "Tara, you're smart sweetie, why don't you become a doctor?" she'd say. Or, "Why not look into being a lawyer?" And lately, it was, "You're the salutatorian of your class, honey, do you really want to take off a year from college?"

For a chance to be a mermaid, the answer to that last question was a resounding 'yes'. It's not a traditional track for the girl who finished second in her class and had scholarship offers from three different universities, yet I had deferred my freshman year to live my dream. After this one year, I could focus on those more sensible things.

If I wanted to.

"How do you breathe underwater?" a young girl asked, tearing me back to reality. She shyly smiled at me and hid behind her mother's skirt. The poor little thing was anxious too, just like me.

"We have to use air tubes," I said with a gracious smile. "So we're able to breathe whenever we want."

"Ariel from *The Little Mermaid* doesn't need air tubes," another girl protested. "She's able to breathe whenever she wants."

I gave a nervous chuckle. I knew it was inevitable that this comparison would come up and I still didn't quite know how to answer it. How do you convince kids that you're a real mermaid when you're not?

"Ariel is a very special mermaid," I said. "She can hold her breath for quite a long time. But we all have to breathe somehow." I winked at her, taking a deep breath to demonstrate my working lungs. The girl giggled, and her parents chuckled as well.

"What's that around your neck?" another girl asked.

As if by instinct, my right hand protectively flew to the pendant that hung around my neck. It was a miniature stone mermaid, carved with startling accuracy and detail. The mermaid had her tail curled around her, her hair flowing like kelp in the sea. It was only about the size of my thumb, yet I cherished it with all my being. After I'd become obsessed with mermaids, my dad gave it to me a few months before he had died of cancer.

I never took it off, even for performances.

"This is a special necklace," I explained and held it out for the kids to see. "It's a mermaid. It was given to me by my father when I was about your age." Strange how even a small mention of it could bring me to the brink of tears. I sniffled, trying to contain it.

I felt a hand on my shoulder. Gratefully, I looked up and saw Christine addressing the crowd. She obviously got the hint that I was getting choked up.

"So many good questions!" she exclaimed. She flashed what I like to call her PR smile. The kids instantly warmed up to her. Even though she was in a turquoise polo shirt and a pair of khaki shorts, she could still command an audience with her ethereal grace like she was wearing her costume. "But Mermaid Tara has to go get ready for her performance at two o'clock."

There were quite a few disappointed groans in the crowd, and that made me smile despite the fact that I was about to tear up.

"Aww, we're sad to see you go too," Christine said, feeding off the crowd. "But we are excited that Mermaid Tara and her friends will be performing a special show just for you right before the dolphin tale show at two o'clock. It's in the Dolphin Stage Arena."

The grumbling got louder as kids and their parents made to leave.

"Okay," Christine said in a low voice so that only I could hear her, putting her hands on her hips. "How did that go for you?"

"All right, I guess," I said. "They got so...curious... towards the end."

Christine smiled. "All it takes is one random question, and then they're *all* asking random questions." She would know. She's been doing this for about ten years and has had countless meet and greets in that time. "I thought you did great, and you made a good impression. Neptune should be happy."

I smiled hopefully.

Neptune was our boss, the owner of Neptune's World Aquarium in Jacksonville, Florida. An old man covered in tattoos on his arm and a white beard on his face, he reminded me of a sailor with his mannerisms and Popeye-like speech. Yet he was a warm and caring man who loved the ocean more than anyone I'd ever met.

We were touring as a troupe of mermaids in aquariums across the country in the winter off-season to generate publicity for Neptune's World. After one stop, it was working: the crowds loved our performances and we were featured online and in the newspapers. Everyone wanted to see the real-life mermaids of Neptune's World. We were now at our second stop at the Houston Aquarium in Texas's largest city.

"You really think he'll be happy?" I asked. It was only my second month working for the aquarium, so I celebrated every little victory I had at making a good impression.

"Yep. All you have left is this show and you'll have had a great day."

I knew I could handle the performance at two. When I was in the water, dancing like a mermaid, I was great. To me, there were no crowds. There were no questions. There was me, the water, and the fullness of heart that only comes with fulfilling a dream.

"All right, let's get me out of here," I said, holding my arms up like a baby wanting to be picked up. "We have a show in an hour."

Christine motioned for the ushers to come help me. While I was in my mermaid tail, there was no way I'd be able to get to the changing room without flopping like a dying fish or some kid seeing me take off my tail.

It was awkward being nearly naked in a strange man's arms as he carried me to the dressing room. At eighteen years old and being what everyone considered the weird kid in high school, I'd never had a real boyfriend. Or any sort of romantic interest really. Not that I'm hideous or anything—at five four, I'm slim with a head full of dark brown hair that falls past my shoulders, green eyes with turquoise flecks that I'd inherited from Dad, and tanned skin from spending way too much time in the sun, so I'd say I had average looks. I wasn't interested in a relationship either. And with me starting my year of professional mermaiding, I seriously doubted I would find a boyfriend now.

By the time we arrived at the changing rooms, I was bright red in the face because the method of transportation was so incredibly awkward. Christine was talking my ear off. She does that sometimes.

"How do you like Houston?" she asked me, her question cutting through my embarrassment.

I blinked at her, refocusing my thoughts on her. "Oh, it's been great."

Granted, we'd only been here for three days and already performed two of those three days, so I hadn't been able to get out and see the city. However, everyone I met had been nice, and both of our performances had been extremely well received. I enjoyed getting out and seeing more of the United States, as I'd been confined to Jacksonville for most of my life.

The usher set me down, and I half-hopped, half-fell over to a chair so I could take off my tail and touch up my make-up before we headed to the Dolphin Stage Arena, where we would perform before they brought out the dolphins for their own show. While we swam with whales and turtles and fish in our usual tank at Neptune's World, we weren't familiar with the animals at the Houston Aquarium, so we were separated into two different performances.

"Hey, Tara, how did your meet and greet go?" a mermaid named Alaina asked. She was in her late twenties, and while she wasn't showing yet, she had announced two weeks ago that she was pregnant and this would be her last season. I liked her a lot, so the thought made me sad.

"Not too great," I admitted.

"Oh, you did fine for your first time," Christine interjected. She went to her mirror and unzipped her own mermaid tail from her garment bag, getting ready herself. "Those kids ask all the darndest questions. I think it's because they all have iPads."

"It's my turn tomorrow," another mermaid, Jordyn said. I glanced at her and I could see her visibly pale at the thought of her first meet and greet. She was only a few years older than me, going to nursing school part-time while she supported herself and her mother with her job as a mermaid.

"We need to think of better answers as to why we don't look and act like Ariel," I explained. "I even got asked why I didn't have red hair."

Jordyn laughed. "At least I have red hair. For the moment."

No kidding. Maybe her Q&A would go better than

mine.

I smirked at my reflection in the mirror. With my over-the-top makeup and the glitter in my hair, I looked the part of an ethereal mermaid. I glanced around at the three other mermaids that were getting ready. We looked like a school of sea nymphs straight from the storybooks.

This was my dream. I was living the life. Sure, there were some moments like my meet and greet where I felt like it was going terribly. Yet to me, this was paradise.

I was checking my phone for messages from my mother when a timid knock at the door caused me to look up. An aquarium volunteer was at the door, smiling shyly.

"You're on in fifteen minutes," she announced.

We had to hurry to the backstage area. It would take us ten minutes simply to get our tails on near the tank where we'd be performing. How we put our tails on was a highly personal ritual. One, because our tails were unique to each of our bodies, and two, because we all had our ways of fitting into the tight silicon, like putting baby powder or lotion on or having help with pulling it up. For me, I had to get into the pool first and then put it on in the water, otherwise it would stick to my dry skin.

"Okay, we'll head out now," Christine said to the volunteer. She looked back and grinned at all of us. "Mermaids, let's do this thing."

ABOUT THE AUTHOR

Sci-fi junkie, video game nerd, and wannabe manga artist Erin Hayes writes a lot of things. Sometimes she writes books, like the fantasy mystery novel Death is but a Dream, the sci-fi middle grade book Jacob Smith is Incredibly Average, and the Her Wolf paranormal series.

She works as an advertising copywriter during the day, and she moonlights as an author. She has lived in New Zealand, Texas, and now in Birmingham, Alabama with her husband, cat, and a growing collection of geek paraphernalia.

You can reach her at erinhayesbooks@gmail. com and she'll be happy to chat. Especially if you want to debate Star Wars.

Made in the USA
Lexington, KY
09 April 2017